Welcome to Temptation

Charlotte Hughes

A Romantic Comedy

Welcome to Temptation was originally published as a *Loveswept* paperback in 1990 by Bantam Books, a division of Bantam, Doubleday, Dell Publishing Group, Inc., under the title *Louisiana Lovin'*. It has since been updated and revised.

Chapter One

The rain fell in earnest, pelting the lush vegetation along the grassy banks of the ever-changing bayou. A bullfrog belched as though protesting the strong gust of wind that shook the tall reeds and Virginia creeper along the riverbank. Fan-shaped palmetto leaves bowed low in the flurry; a carpet of duckweed was swept to one side of the bayou, where it nestled among knobby cypress knees and flowering water hyacinths. Overhead, the August sky hung like a giant water-filled canopy about to burst. A blast of wind sent water spraying through an open window, and Michelle Thurston slammed it closed.

She tossed her grandmother a look of pure annoyance. "Reba Kenner, you are the most stubborn, hard-headed, obstinate woman I ever laid eyes on. You're a dead woman, you know that? If you stay here, you're as good as dead."

The elderly woman obliged her granddaughter

with a smile and a nod. At eighty, Reba Kenner was a shrunken version of her former self. But her skin was smooth and free of mottling and her nappy white hair clean and healthy looking, the result of a concoction she'd drank for years that she declared was part bayou water. It was the same remedy she'd insisted her granddaughter drink as a teenager to ward off acne and was the reason, or so Reba said, that at thirty, Michelle's complexion was flawless and her long ash-blond hair thick and luscious. But if Michelle looked anxious, her grandmother was anything but.

"Would you like more coffee now, dear?" she asked at last in a pleasant, fruity-textured voice.

Michelle fixed her green-eyed gaze on her grandmother, her anxiety and frustration mounting, much as the wind outside had in the past hour. "Have you even heard a word I've said, Grand?" she demanded.

"I heard most of it," the woman confessed, "but I may as well tell you the battery is going dead on my hearing aid, and I haven't replaced it. I thought maybe we'd go into town while you're here."

Michelle stared at the woman in disbelief. "We can't go to town," she said, raising her voice, hoping her grandmother could hear. "We're under a hurricane warning!"

"Yes, I heard it on the news. They're calling it Katie, you know."

"That's right. And it wiped out part of Cuba last night. Do you understand? It's probably going to wipe us out too." Michelle resisted the urge to shake her grandmother as she spoke—anything to make her see reason. Since her parents were out of town on business, as usual, it was up to her to see to her grandmother, which, under normal circumstances was a pleasure. They had always been close. But she was exhausted, having pulled the graveyard shift in the emergency room the night before, during which time she'd made periodic checks on the storm's progress. At five a.m. it had changed course, and the small town of Temptation, Louisiana was right in its path. Because Reba had no use for telephones, Michelle wasn't able to call. If they survived the storm, she was going to insist Reba have one installed.

She'd made the two-hour drive from Baton Rouge in record time, arriving shortly after nine that morning, still wearing her nurse's uniform. Now, she was tempted to throw the slight woman over her shoulder and run for her car before their time ran out.

Reba stroked the gold tabby in her lap. The cat purred loudly and curled into a fat ball. "I'm not leaving my animals, Mic," she said, her eyes suddenly bright with tears.

Michelle had only seen her grandmother cry once, and that had been at her grandfather's funeral. Seeing them now was as traumatic as some of the scenes she faced in the emergency room. She felt her own eyes sting at the sight as she glanced about helplessly at the menagerie of animals. Two more cats sprawled on the old-fashioned braided rug in front of the fireplace. In the kitchen, a blue-tick hound named Mae West had recently given birth to six puppies. A large antique birdcage in the dining room held a green parrot named Mister Ed, who hadn't stopped squawking since Michelle arrived.

"I suppose we could take them to Baton Rouge with us," she said, although she did not relish the thought of hauling a small zoo in her brand new BMW. She had saved every spare dime for three years in order to afford it. And to think, she'd paid extra for the pearl colored leather seats.

Reba chuckled. "I can just see all that fur a-flyin'," she said. "That hound won't let anybody or anything within six feet of those puppies."

Michelle sighed heavily and sank onto an old wicker rocker that matched nothing else in the room. Reba's house had always looked as though it had been furnished from a neighborhood garage sale. She threw nothing away. Everything in the house was either patched or mended, but Michelle, who preferred newer styles, had to admit the furniture was very comfortable. What she'd give to curl up and take a nap on her grandmother's vintage iron bed.

"I should have known you'd fight me over this," Michelle said tiredly. "What am I going to do with you, Grand? You've become such a recluse since grandpa died. How is anybody supposed to know if you're sick or injured, for Pete's sake?"

Reba reached over and patted her granddaughter's hand affectionately. "I can take care of myself, dear, really I can. And you know how much I like my privacy." She made a tsking sound. "You're just tired. You always did turn into a fussy little thing when you got sleepy. Why don't you lie down on the sofa and rest? This old house is a lot stronger than you think. Why, I've ridden out more storms in this place than I can remember. And so have you, if you'll think back over the summers you spent here as a child. It even made it through Katrina. We'll be safe."

Michelle knew it was useless to argue. When Reba made up her mind, no one could change it. She could beg and plead but it would only fuel Reba's determination to stay. "I suppose we should get the house ready," Michelle said at last, pulling herself up from the rocker. She didn't know where to begin. She was trained to handle emergencies—it was what she did best. But most folks cooperated in tense situations, and Reba was doing her best not to.

Michelle tried to think of everything they might

need if the storm hit hard—and she feared it would after hearing all the destruction it had caused thus far. It had picked up speed and turned due north. It was scheduled to hit Pensacola, Biloxi, and New Orleans that afternoon.

And then she heard it. At first Michelle thought it was the wind, but the grinding noise persisted. She hurried over to the window, wiped the steamy glass with the ball of her hand, and peered out. A small motorboat, barely visible in the rain, rounded the bend of cypress trees. "Somebody's coming," she said.

"In this weather?" Reba pushed herself up from the chair and joined her granddaughter at the window. "Oh, that'd be Gator Landry," she said. "He's our new sheriff," she added. "'Course, Gator ain't his real name. He was named Mathieu after his daddy. But folks 'round here have always called him Gator. I don't reckon I know why."

Michelle's eyes widened to the size of half-dollars. "Not the Gator Landry I met the summer I turned sixteen!" she said. Dumb question. How many Gator Landry's could there be in one small town? She remembered the wild, black-haired, black-eyed Cajun who'd teased and tormented and pursued her unmercifully that summer. "Somebody actually made him sheriff?"

"Aw, Gator's okay," Reba said. "I reckon he's got a wild hair in him, but if he turns out half as well as his daddy, he'll be a good man. His daddy was sheriff for many years, you know." Reba paused. "'Course Gator wasn't none too pleased when the folks here 'lected him. He put up quite a stink. He'd made a little money on a sugar cane plantation south of here and had his heart set on taking it easy for a while. Yes, it really riled him when they made him sheriff."

Michelle pressed her lips into a grim line. "Why'd he take the job?"

Reba shrugged. "This town's been good to Gator's family. Their house burned to the ground when he was just a young'un, and a bunch of people got together and built them a new place. Gator's mother still lives there, and while he was gone all those years making his fortune, the folks here looked after her. Besides, our last sheriff wasn't worth a cuss. He'd just sit back and let that wild bunch from the pool hall terrorize folks. I s'pect he was scared of 'em. Anyway, the town booted him out and 'lected Gator sheriff. Everybody knows that Gator Landry ain't scared of nothin' or nobody." She chuckled. "He raised hell, though; when he found out they'd voted him in without his permission."

"He could have gotten out of it," Michelle said, "if he was that much against it."

Reba's smile drooped, and her look turned serious. "He probably would have walked away had somebody not attacked his mama and stolen her purse. She fought back and ended up in the hospital with a concussion. It was pretty scary, shook Gator up something fierce. You never know what to expect with a concussion, but I don't have to tell you that."

"Is she okay?"

"She healed up real good, but let me tell you what —" Reba paused and looked at the ceiling. "Once she was out of danger, Gator went on a manhunt. He headed straight for the pool hall, and when the owner refused to unlock the door—I reckon he knew Gator was out for blood—Gator kicked it in. The owner told Gator that the man who robbed his mama did not know who she was at the time of the robbery, but once he found out he left town. Just picked up in the middle of the night and took off."

"Smart guy," Michelle said.

"Yes, indeed. No telling what Gator would have done to him. Gator closed down the pool hall. 'Course, the owner has friends in high places so he was back in business in a couple of days. But don't think he don't know that Gator is watching his every move. Just watching and waiting. Soon as somebody messes up, Gator is going to be on them like white on rice, as my mama used to say."

Michelle shook her head. Gator Landry was one of the last people she'd have expected to run into after all these years. Of course, it was bound to happen sooner or later in a town the size of Temptation, where almost everybody was related by blood or marriage. "Why do you suppose he's here?" Michelle asked, watching the man in a bright yellow slicker tie his boat securely to the small pier at the back of Reba's house, no easy task now that the wind had picked up. Even from a distance she could tell that his chest and shoulders had broadened over the years.

Reba gave a grunt. "He's gonna try and make me leave, that's what. But I ain't budgin'." Reba threw open the back door and leaned out. "Get in this house, Gator!" she yelled, obviously trying to make herself heard above the wind and rain. "You gonna drown out there in that weather."

For a moment, the only sound Michelle heard other than the wind was her own heartbeat. She chided herself for the attack of nerves. Heavens, she and Gator had been mere teenagers the last time they'd seen each other. He probably would not remember her.

Gator climbed the steps to the back porch and paused, shrugging out of his rain gear before he joined Reba inside. He gave her a hug, then glanced Michelle's way. His hair and eyes were still black as crows' feathers, only she saw the whites of his eyes were bloodshot. His jaw was scruffy and the clothes he wore disheveled, as though he'd slept in them. He turned his gaze back to Reba. Michelle was relieved that he had not recognized her.

"I guess you heard the storm turned on us," he said, his deep voice seasoned with an accent that was uniquely Cajun. "I have to get you out of here. We're settin' up shelters in town."

"I'm not going, Gator," Reba said, hitching her chin stubbornly. "You know they won't let me bring my animals into those shelters, and I refuse to leave them defenseless. Besides, my granddaughter will take care of me."

Gator glanced Michelle's way once again, only this time he paused. Their gazes collided. For a moment, they merely stared at each other, and the silence that followed was as deafening as the wind and rain outside. "What are you doing here?" he asked, his tone almost accusing.

His abrupt manner surprised her. So he did remember her, Michelle told herself, giving none of her own thoughts away in her cool appraisal. The years had been good to him. He was still handsome in a rough-around-the-edges sort of way. Perhaps *striking* was a better word. His nose and mouth were a bit pronounced, an indication of his heritage, but while those same features might appear unsightly on another man's face, they added character to his.

Michelle suddenly found her voice. "Hello, Gator," she said. "I thought my grandmother might need me ... what with the storm coming and all."

"You two shouldn't be here," he said. "This storm is right on our tails now. I've got to get you to safety. Everyone else has already evacuated or sought shelter."

"That's what I've been preaching since I arrived," Michelle said. "To no avail," she added.

"I'm not going anywhere," Reba said. Gator and Michelle suddenly looked her way, as though they'd forgotten she was in the room. "Besides, I ain't scared of no storm," Reba added, crossing her wiry arms over her bosom.

Gator sighed heavily and raked his fingers through his dark hair. Damn, but his head hurt. He probably had the worst hangover of his life. This storm was the last thing he needed. "Now, Reba, don't put up a fuss," he said. "When this hurricane hits it's going to rip this place apart, and you won't be able to help yourself, much less those animals. Come get in the boat before it fills up with water and sinks."

"I ain't goin', Gator, and that's final." Reba marched over to her rocking chair and sat down stiffly. Her look was unyielding.

"Then I'm going to pick you up and haul you out to the boat, chair and all," he said, his look as ominous as the approaching storm.

Reba gripped the arms of the chair. "And I'll kick and scream this house down over our heads," she said.

"Oh, yeah?" Gator planted his hands on his hips and glared at the woman.

She fixed him with a stubborn gaze. "Yeah."

Michelle looked from one to the other. Watching them interact would have been amusing had the circumstances not been so dire. Her grandmother was a tiny figure compared to Gator's six-foot-plus frame. The khaki-colored shirt he wore strained against his wide chest, upon which a gold sheriff's badge had been pinned. His faded jeans molded to his thighs and calves like a leather glove. She saw no sign of a gun, but that didn't mean he wasn't armed. He was certainly different from the men she worked with, who wore neat slacks and crisp white lab coats.

Reba gave a harrumph. "You wouldn't shoot an old lady."

"Don't count on it," he said.

"Let her be," Michelle said.

One pair of black eyes snapped up in surprise as Michelle closed the distance between herself and Gator. She had never forgotten those onyx eyes. They could pierce a stone wall and turn a woman's knees to gelatin at the same time.

"You can't force her to go with you," Michelle said, "and all the threats in the world aren't going to change her mind."

Despite his ever-souring mood, Gator looked amused. "Aw, Reba knows I won't really shoot her," he said. "I could just give her a good pistol whipping."

"I'll stay with her."

His look turned to disbelief. Michelle Thurston hadn't lost her spunk, thank goodness, but what she was suggesting was shear lunacy. "You're going to ride out the storm with Reba?" he asked.

"We've ridden out more than one storm in this old house."

"Perhaps you haven't heard how big this thing is," Gator replied.

"I've been listening to weather reports."

He looked about. "Well, then, I take it you have all the supplies you need?"

Michelle did not respond. She had not brought supplies because she'd had no intention of staying. She had planned to help her grandmother pack a few things and hit the road. "I was in the process of getting things together when you showed up." Michelle preferred lying to him than appearing foolish. "I'm sure we'll be fine," she said. "In the meantime, you're probably needed in town."

"Are you trying to get rid of me?" He did not wait for her to reply. "You know, if I weren't such a nice guy, I could handcuff the two of you and haul you to jail for not following evacuation orders."

"Really?" Michelle folded her arms in front of her. "And I could probably call this attorney I know and have you kicked out of office."

"You would do that for me?" Gator asked, sounding delighted. "That's the best offer I've had in a long time."

"Now, now, children," Reba admonished gently. "Let's don't bicker. We're just tense because of the storm." She pulled herself out of her rocker. "Come on in the kitchen, Gator, and let me give you something to eat. You look awful. You must've had a late night."

"Don't go trying to change the subject on me, Reba." He followed her into the next room. "But I will take a glass of tomato juice if you have it. And a couple of aspirin," he added.

Michelle stood there dumbfounded. She followed them and watched from the kitchen door as Gator accepted the aspirin and washed it down with a tall glass of tomato juice.

"I don't believe this," she said. "You have a hangover. No wonder your eyes are so bloodshot. You look as though you just crawled out of some woman's bed. Is that a hickey on your neck, for heaven's sake?"

"Michelle!" Reba said. "That is no way to treat a guest."

Gator set his empty glass on the kitchen table and faced Michelle, clearly annoyed. "It's nobody's business how I spend my Saturday nights. Now, could we stop harping on my personal life and get the hell out of here? I don't have all day."

When Reba spoke, she was adamant. "This is the last time I'm going to tell you, Gator: I ain't going."

He regarded the older woman for a moment. "If you won't think about yourself, think about your granddaughter. Are you willing to put her life in danger as well?"

Reba was clearly shaken at the thought. She had obviously been so wrapped up in saving the lives of her pets that she hadn't considered Michelle or herself. Her face crumpled and sudden tears filled her eyes. "Then make her go with you, Gator."

"Don't be ridiculous, Grand," Michelle said. "I'm not leaving you." She took one spindly hand in her own. "We'll be okay," she told the woman, sounding a lot braver than she felt; but she had to admit, in all honesty, if the tables were turned and someone told her she would have to leave her pets behind, she wouldn't have been able to do it either.

Gator looked from one woman to the other. It was obvious Michelle was trying to get rid of him. Impatience and anxiety were written all over her pretty face and magnified in those emerald green eyes. Lord, those eyes! He could see forever when he looked into them. And that hair. It was just as he remembered, yellow with just a hint of red, a color that emphasized her rosy, unblemished complexion. He could still remember how silky it felt against his bare chest. Aw, damn, he thought. That was the last thing he needed to think about.

Gator shoved his thoughts aside. He had to concentrate on protecting them. He was the sheriff, it was his duty. It didn't matter, at least for the time being, that he didn't want the job, had never wanted the job, for that matter. Until he found somebody capable of taking his place, it was his responsibility. They were his responsibility.

Gator muttered a string of four-letter words under his breath as he considered the situation. He finally gave a huge sigh. "Okay, Reba, we'll do it your way," he said. "I don't suppose you have any extra plywood lying around? Or is that too much to hope for?"

The abrupt change of subject surprised both women. "I reckon there's some under the house," Reba said. "No telling how long it has been under there. Why?"

"I'm going to have to board up these windows," he said, motioning to the large plate-glass windows that dominated the back of the house, "as well as other larger-sized ones, especially on the first floor. A strong wind could shatter the glass or toss something right through it." He gave an inward sigh. Nothing like waiting till the damn storm was right on your butt to start taking precautions, he thought as he stepped out onto the porch and pulled on his boots and slicker. He looked at Michelle standing in the doorway. "See if you can find me a hammer and nails."

"You're staying?" she said in disbelief, knowing he probably had a long list of things to do in town.

"I'm sure as hell not leaving the two of you out here alone," he said, already heading toward the back steps.

Michelle watched him go. "I should have known something like this was going to happen," she said to her grandmother. "Better tell me where the hammer is. I don't think we're going to get rid of him."

Gator found the plywood stacked neatly under the back of the house. He muttered another string of curses when he realized he'd have to crawl a good distance to reach it. He grunted in frustration as he dropped to his belly and shimmied beneath the house toward the stack of plywood. Why had he let them pin that badge to him in the first place, he asked himself, not for the first time. Hadn't he paid his dues where hard work was concerned? Lord, he'd sweated in those sugar cane fields for ten years before he'd turned a profit. He'd gone without material things, had learned to live on next to nothing, just to put every dime back into the crop. And it had paid off.

He could afford to live anywhere he desired. He no longer had to deny himself life's simplest pleasures. He would answer to no one, nor try to prove himself. He could give his mother a better life, pay someone to do the chores she was finding increasingly difficult, and if she became ill he could afford any doctor. He could do for her those things that his father, despite his high opinion of himself, could not have done.

Then a bunch of old fools had gone behind his back and elected him sheriff.

Of course, he would keep the job until he found out who'd beat up his mother, just in case the person had not left town and was only laying low for a while. Once he took care of that piece of business, and he would take care of it, he'd resign and be done with it.

But first he had to get through this emergency. It was a massive bump in the road he hadn't expected, but despite being irritated as hell, he had to take care of Reba. Not to mention that granddaughter of hers who obviously thought herself too good for the likes of him. The young lady must have a short memory, he thought. There was a time, when, had he put forth a little more effort, he could have had her right where he wanted. He wondered if Michelle had ever stopped long enough to consider it.

Had he gone after her that night ... but he hadn't. At sixteen, she'd been too fresh and too new, a tiny bud about to bloom. She'd made him think of everything that was good and decent, and at eighteen years old he had nothing to offer. She had more living and more learning to do before someone took that from her, and, although someone surely would, he wouldn't be that person.

Michelle, draped in her raincoat, hurried out back in search of Gator. The rain fell in sheets. The wind slapped her coat against her legs and spit mud onto the slacks of her nurses' uniform. She cautiously crossed the backyard, trying not to slip in the wet grass. She found Gator sprawled beneath the back of the house. For a moment, all she could do was stare. His slicker had worked its way up around his waist, exposing his jean-clad body from the hips down. And how about those hips, she thought, her gaze fastened to the taut muscles. Her eyes lingered just a moment before moving downward to his lean thighs and calves. And then all at once, those hips started moving, sliding from side to side like a rattlesnake in reverse. There was a loud grunt, and the rest of his body emerged, his big fists gripping several sheets of plywood.

"Well, don't just stand there," Gator said, once he'd spied her. "Help me get this plywood out. And when we're done with this batch, there is more beneath the other side of the house."

"You don't have to be mean," she said. "I've done nothing to deserve it." She set the hammer and box of nails under the house so they wouldn't get wet. She stooped beside him and pulled the plywood out. It was going to be a long day, she thought.

Several hours later, Michelle and Gator had

managed to board up the largest windows on the back of the house, although it was next to impossible to work against the fierce wind. Several times Michelle found herself flattened against the house, unable to move because of the wind's force, while the screens billowed and strained with each gust. One tore loose and spit rain into her face, almost blinding her. Finally, Gator gripped her around the waist with both arms and literally shoved her toward the back door.

"Go inside," he yelled, "before the wind picks you up and tosses you into the bayou."

Michelle didn't argue. She knew she'd only hinder him further because of her inability to fight the wind. She managed to get the back door open, but another wind gust sent water spraying onto the wood floor and onto Reba, who helped close the door behind Michelle.

"Where'd Gator run off to?" she asked, wringing her frail hands.

"He should be here momentarily," Michelle said, gasping for breath. "It's bad out there, Grand. Real bad." Michelle noticed for the first time that Reba's hound was standing beside her. "What is Mae West doing out of bed? Shouldn't she be with her puppies?"

"The wind scared her." Reba said. "She can't sit still. And Mister Ed is going bananas." She motioned toward the parrot, whose claws gripped the side of his cage as he squawked.

"I need all the masking and duct tape you can get your hands on," Michelle told her grandmother. "While I tape the small windows I want you to look for candles. Oh, and a couple of spare flashlights would help."

Michelle shrugged out of her raincoat but didn't bother to get out of her wet uniform. She went right to work, taping windows as fast as she could. Gator came in a few minutes later and assisted. By the time they ran out of tape they'd managed to secure most of the windows on the first floor, as well as the larger ones on the second.

Gator backed away from one of the large plate-glass windows in an upper-story bedroom and surveyed the big X's they'd made on the glass with masking tape. "I suppose that's the best we can do on such short notice."

Michelle saw that he was literally soaked to the skin. His jeans were plastered against his thighs and calves in a way that made her mouth go dry. His shirt was drenched as well and hung open to his waist, exposing his wide chest, where black hair glistened wetly. His thick hair was slicked to his scalp, giving him a rakish appearance. Michelle realized that she didn't look much better. Her uniform was saturated, and it molded to her body like a second skin. Her nipples, erect from the cold rain and chafing the cotton material of her uniform, were clearly visible as they strained against the wet fabric. She blushed profusely when she caught Gator staring. But if she was uncomfortable before, it was nothing compared to the unease she felt when those hooded black eyes locked with her own.

"We need to get out of these wet things," she said, crossing her arms in front of her in an attempt to hide herself. She shivered as Gator continued to stare. He still had the power to make her body go berserk when he looked at her that way, she thought. Those glittering black eyes didn't miss a thing. It was as though he were capable of seeing past flesh and bone to her inner workings, all of which shook at the moment as violently as the tree limbs outside the window. She was certain he knew what that look did to her—what it did to every female, for that matter. He had it down to an art. And if it had had a powerful effect on her at sixteen, it was doubly so now at thirty-two.

"That's the best idea I've heard all day," Gator said, shrugging out of his shirt. It was cold and felt like wet seaweed against his skin. He mopped his brow and chest with it and ran it across the back of his neck.

Michelle wondered if he had any idea how sensual that simple act was. He was all rippling muscles and taut flesh. Goose pimples stood out on his shoulders and his nipples puckered from the chill in the room. His arms were lean and as brown as the rest of him. The room seemed to shrink in size. Michelle had seen enough male bodies in her job to know that the one before her was one of the best she'd ever laid eyes on.

Gator would have had to be blind not to notice her perusal. The grin he shot her was brazen. "Like what you see, Mic?"

Michelle's head snapped up with a force that almost sent her reeling. Her face flamed. "I was just ... just ..."

"Staring?" He looked faintly amused.

He was laughing at her, she thought angrily. She fought the urge to race out of the room. "Don't flatter yourself," she said.

"You've still got the prettiest green eyes I've ever seen. Not to mention the cutest rear end. I'd say you have improved with age." He slung his damp shirt around his neck and stepped closer. "So you're a nurse now. I remember the first time you told me you wanted to go into nursing. Do you?"

Michelle fought the urge to back away from him. To do so would have been cowardly, and she would sooner bite off her tongue than show Gator she was afraid of him. "How can I forget," she said. "You suggested we play doctor so I could practice on you."

He chuckled. "But you refused."

"That's because I knew what ailed you and didn't want any part of it."

"I think you did. Had we been older maybe things would have turned out differently."

"I see you haven't lost your arrogance," she said.

"You're still crazy about me, aren't you?"

She almost laughed, because at the moment it was just like old times, with Gator trying his darnedest to get a rise out of her and her tossing his words or innuendos right back in his face. Gator Landry had always been able to make her blush and feel things that other boys couldn't.

"I was only sixteen years old at the time. I'm twice that age now, and I hope I've got twice the sense I had back then when I acted on hormones instead of common sense. Besides, you weren't the first man to kiss me; nor the last."

He cocked his head to the side, as though pondering the thought. "Maybe not, but I'll bet I'm the one you remember best."

She wished he wouldn't stand so close. Every nerve in her body was alive with anticipation, and if that anticipation had been sweet at sixteen, it was even more so now that she fully understood where all those feelings and sensations led. She was sensitized to his every move—the way his chest rose and fell, the way his dark lashes fluttered when he blinked, and the way his warm breath felt on her cheek.

"You know we could all die out here, Mic," he said, his dark gaze resting on her lips. "In about another hour, this storm could blow us clear to kingdom come. What d'you say we give each other a little present?"

Michelle didn't know if he was serious or not, but her mouth flew open in surprise at his blatant request. Gator took it as an invitation, and his own mouth suddenly opened over hers, capturing it in a warm kiss. His big arms snaked around her waist and pulled her close, so close that she could feel the hard muscles of his thighs pressing against hers, the wall of his chest crushing her breasts.

The years had not erased the taste of him from her memory. His tongue coaxed her mouth open wider, making gentle forays between her lips that sent her head spinning. His palms slid down the small of her back, cupped each hip, and pulled her tighter against him, cradling her against the base of his thighs, where his arousal was more than evident. Had another man done the same thing, it would have seemed indecent and out of place, but for a man like Gator, it was as much a part of the kiss as his lips. Gator did nothing halfway. And Michelle could only stand there and hang on for dear life, praying her knees would not buckle beneath her.

When he finally raised his head, he was smiling.

"Nothing has changed between us, Mic," he said with his voice soft with invitation. "After all these years, I still want you. Just as badly as I did when you were sixteen and didn't really know what you were doing. Its better when you're older, you know. But this time I refuse to stop after a few hot kisses."

Michelle realized she was gasping, and she had to wonder if Gator's kisses were more dangerous than anything the storm could do to her.

Chapter Two

By noon, the fierce wind howled and shrieked like a wild animal, and the house shuddered with each violent gust. Dressed in dry clothes that Reba had pulled from an upstairs closet, Gator dickered with a battery-powered radio that produced a great deal of static. He'd muttered a few curses under his breath when he realized he'd left his police radio back at the shelter. Not that it would have done much good anyway since he was so far out in the bayou country. He was going to insist that Reba get a telephone after this thing was over. At her age, with her car running only half the time, she had to have some way of contacting people. It was too easy to forget about her living out here all alone, and he wouldn't always be around to remind folks.

Michelle, wearing pants that were too big and had to be pinned at the waist, gazed through a partially boarded window where the trees outside shook and swayed, as though some great Pandora's box had been opened and had unleashed something awful and evil. Tree limbs and debris were tossed against the house, and then sucked in another direction. Her ears popped suddenly, signaling a change in pressure that was as frightening as the wind outside.

Gator stepped closer, still holding the radio at his ear. “Better come away from that window,” he said. He’d barely gotten the words out of his mouth before something hit the house with force; it felt as though it had been lifted momentarily from its foundation. Reba, who’d been rocking in her chair frantically for the past hour, stopped and glanced up as the lights flickered once and went out. They were shrouded in near darkness.

“The water is rising fast,” Gator said, going to the window that he’d ordered Michelle away from only seconds before. Reba joined him..

“It looks like the end of the world,” she said softly, holding a small calico kitten. She looked from Gator to her granddaughter and back, and she appeared to be on the verge of tears. “You were right. We shouldn’t have stayed. If anything happens to the two of you, it’ll be all my fault.”

“Nothing’s going to happen,” Gator said, anchoring his hands on her frail shoulders reassuringly.

Michelle would’ve had to be deaf not to catch the gravity of his voice. Once again, she stepped closer to the window. They were drawn to it like moths to a porch light. She tossed Gator an anxious look over her grandmother's head and found him watching her, a thoughtful expression on his face. She wondered what he was thinking. Was he sorry now for staying? She suddenly remembered the kiss they'd shared and glanced away quickly. She returned her gaze to the window, where the bayou, usually without current, was now a pulsing, moving thing with ripples and whitecaps. It reminded her of the way her stomach pitched about each time Gator looked at her with those black eyes.

Gator finally insisted they move to the center of the room, away from the windows. For the next couple of hours they waited and listened as reports filtered in on the radio, although some of it was interrupted with bouts of static. They lunched on ham and cheese sandwiches and spice cake and made small talk as they listened and waited. Time crept by slowly while Reba rocked and quietly hummed church hymns. Gator tried to pull Michelle into conversation.

"Remember the time we got caught in that storm at the swimming hole?" he asked.

Michelle slid her gaze in his direction and felt her face grow warm at the memory. "No."

The smile he gave her told her he knew she was lying. "Think for a minute. It'll come back to you. It started lightning, and we had to leave the water."

How could she forget, she wanted to rail at him. She had ended up in the front seat of his old pickup truck, alone with him, wearing only her bathing suit and smelling of suntan lotion. Something in her stomach fluttered as she remembered how he'd looked in his bathing trunks that day.

Gator had matured much faster than the rest of the boys his age, and that day, with his naked chest glistening with oil and his wet trunks clinging to him, Michelle had been convinced of that maturity. That was the day Gator had kissed her for the first time, though heaven knew he'd tried a dozen times before. She couldn't remember exactly how it had begun, but all at once she'd found him close, his mouth touching hers tentatively, as if he were half-afraid she'd scurry away like the squirrels had when the rain had begun. But she hadn't. She had raised her lips to his eagerly. That one kiss awakened everything in her body, those gentle stirrings that he had aroused in her the first time she'd seen him. She had touched his chest, had drawn tiny playful circles in the light coating of oil that covered him, and had watched in wonder as his nipples had contracted. She had lain in bed that night for hours, thinking about it, wondering what it would have been like had she not put a halt to the kissing that in just a few minutes had grown hot and frantic. And then she'd buried her head under her pillow and squeezed her eyes tightly closed, trying to convince herself that no sixteen-year-old girl should ever feel the things Gator had made her feel.

"Yes, I remember," she finally said, meeting the look in his eyes. She wondered if he knew how powerful that look was. It was almost hypnotic. She felt as though she were being pulled toward him, like a small fish being reeled in on a line. "It seems so long ago," she added, thinking out loud. She wondered how it could still be so vivid.

"Sometimes it seems like yesterday," he said.

Something slammed against the side of the house, and Michelle jumped as reality closed in with an urgency that made her tremble. The noise heightened, until the whole area sounded like a war zone. Water lapped onto the back porch and seeped under the back door. They tried in vain to mop it up with towels. Mister Ed squawked and flapped his wings while the hound paced the floor nervously. And then, just when Michelle thought she could take no more, the wind and rain stopped and all she could hear was her own frantic heartbeat. All three hurried over to the window and gazed out at the carnage of small trees and limbs and debris. Everything was dead still. She looked at Gator. "Is it over?"

Gator shook his head. "'Fraid not, Mic. I think it's just the eye passing over."

She liked the way he said her pet name; it always came out sounding like "Meek." She remembered a magnolia-scented night when he'd whispered her name in her ear, his breath hot against her cheek. She'd sneaked out with him on a dare. She remembered him pulling her down beside him on his mother's old-fashioned quilt, a light summer breeze toying with her hair and fanning her body. His usual playful manner had disappeared that night; the teasing was gone. He'd been a man filled with such a passionate need that it had frightened her.

Suddenly, they were no longer mere teenagers experimenting with touch and feel. The slow burning in Michelle's lower belly had blazed into something wild and reckless, teetering out of control. It had jolted her to the soles of her feet. No boy had ever made her feel those things. She had run from him, leapt from the blanket and torn through the woods as though the devil himself were after her. She had slipped back into her grandparents' house soundlessly, but her heart was beating so loud that she'd been half-afraid the walls would come crashing down around her. It would serve her right, she'd told herself over and over. No decent girl would slip out at midnight to be with the likes of Gator Landry.

That was the last time she'd seen him, and she was almost thankful when her parents had come for her the next day. She'd put the summer and her three-month relationship with Gator Landry behind her. She'd never even told him good bye. But she'd figured it was just as well. Gator probably hated her for running away from him. Or perhaps he'd had a good laugh over it with his friends. She'd vowed not to humiliate herself further where he was concerned.

Michelle forced her thoughts back to the present. Another few minutes passed in absolute silence before Gator decided to venture outside and have a look around. She followed, wearing rubber knee boots to keep dry. Nothing moved. The air was heavy and oppressive, so thick, Michelle was certain she could chew it. They rounded the house and she gasped, finding a great live oak completely unearthed, lying across the back of her new BMW. Her heart sank.

"Well, there goes all hope of getting out of here, she said, feeling the sting of tears at her eyes. She and Gator stepped closer to survey the damage.

He shook his head but tried to sound optimistic. "Good thing it didn't fall on the front of your car, or it would have crushed your engine."

Michelle laughed hollowly. "What does that matter? It's still a wreck and I just-bought the damn thing." She was crying now, but she didn't care. "I special-ordered that color and had to wait two months to get it. All those months of doing without, saving every dime I could get my hands on. Giving up my vacation days," she added on a heartfelt sob.

Gator's gut clinched at the sight of her tears. He could stand anything but a woman's tears. "Aw, Mic, don't cry." He draping one arm over her shoulder. "We're lucky to be alive. I can get somebody out here to pull that tree off your car. You can take it to a body shop, and they'll have it looking brand new again. Just be thankful it was your car and not one of us."

Michelle couldn't stop crying no matter how hard she tried. "We could still die," she said, swiping at the tears miserably. "The back side of the storm is supposed to be as bad as the front, if not worse. If something happens to Grand, I'll never forgive myself for not putting my foot down and forcing her to leave."

"I think she had her mind made up," he said softly. "It wouldn't be anybody's fault."

Michelle hiccupped. "Oh, Gator, I'm so scared. I've never been this scared in my life. I'm used to seeing unpleasant things. I see them every day as part of my job. But this is different. The whole house could fall down around us. We could—" She paused and shook her head.

"Don't think like that, Mic," he said gently. "We've taken every precaution."

Nevertheless, tears streamed down her cheeks, fear and exhaustion warring inside her. She closed her eyes, trying to block out the images around her.

Gator hugged her close, feeling his heart swell with genuine concern. “You’re one of the bravest women I know,” he said at last. “And I’m not going to let this thing hurt you or your grandmother. I’ll do anything to keep you safe. Do you understand?”

Michelle opened her eyes. For once there was no sign of laughter or amusement on his face. His look was both tender and sincere. It felt wonderful in his arms, she decided. Secure. She felt safe for the first time in hours. As crazy as it sounded, she did trust him, and she knew he would do anything to prevent them from getting hurt.

“Sometimes, I get tired of being brave all the time,” she confessed. “People come into the emergency room looking so bad, it’s all I can do not to turn and run in the other direction.” She swallowed a lump at the back of her throat. “They look at us as if we’ve got the power to make them live and—” She stopped. “We don’t always. They beg us not to let them die, their families beg us to keep them alive, but sometimes we just can’t.”

“You can only do so much,” he said, smoothing her hair back from her face with a big hand. Gator couldn’t believe the feeling of tenderness that had welled up in him over her confession. She had always seemed so self-assured, so in control of her feelings. That was one of the reasons he had always enjoyed teasing her. He wanted to see if he could crack that cool exterior, make that wall of reserve come tumbling down around her. He had teased and tormented and tried his damnedest to seduce her even though he knew better, but he'd never stood by and watched her heart seemingly break into a million pieces. It suddenly became of the utmost importance to protect her and Reba.

Michelle squirmed deeper into his embrace and closed her eyes again, unaware of the effect she was having on him. It had been so long since she'd been held by a man. Everybody needed to be hugged, or simply touched by another human being from time to time, she told herself. She gave so much of herself to her patients; was it wrong to ask for something for herself? She slipped her arms around Gator's waist, and pressed herself against his solid body, wishing to draw upon his strength.

She had spent so many years offering strength and nurturing others that it felt wonderful receiving the same back. The storm would return with all its fury before long, and they could very well die, but for now she wanted to bask in the warmth of Gator's embrace. Nothing else mattered at the moment. She was obviously in shock, she told herself. People did strange things when faced with their own mortality. But she forced the thought away, focusing instead on his scent and the way his lips felt in her hair and against her forehead as he tried to offer comfort.

"Kiss me, Gator," she said, her voice a mere

whisper.

He needed no further prompting. Gator lowered his head and captured her lips. Michelle remained as still as the world around them as his warm mouth opened over hers. His tongue was hot as it forged past her lips and explored her mouth with a thoroughness that left her tingling inside and out. His hands moved to the small of her back, caressing and kneading the tense muscles there while the muscles low in her belly coiled tightly. She opened her eyes slowly when Gator raised his head.

"We'd better go back in now," he said. He wanted her more than he'd ever wanted her as a teen, but he could not afford to lose his head. He had promised to protect her and Reba, and he had every intention of doing just that. "Your grandmother will be worried."

Michelle nodded dumbly, and they headed for the house. She knew it was just a matter of time before they caught the backlash of the storm.

#

The second half of the storm, which seemed to go on forever, shattered windows, snapped trees in half, and a surge dumped water throughout the first floor of the house. Gator, having foreseen the event, had ordered both women upstairs into a short hall where there were no windows. Reba had insisted on bringing the animals up as well, so they huddled together in silence while Mister Ed squawked from his cage, the cats slinked from room to room, and Mae West growled menacingly from her box filled with puppies. Their only light was provided by an old kerosene lamp. Sometime later they dined on cold pork and beans and cornbread. From time to time, Gator shined his flashlight down the stairwell.

Michelle had avoided talking to him as much as possible once her fear had abated and common sense had returned, along with the jolting realization that she had asked Gator to kiss her. Good grief, she still couldn't believe it! This was a man who no doubt spent his Saturday nights staring into a beer bottle and playing musical beds with any woman who was willing, she reminded herself, and she had played right into his arms. Surely he realized she had been near hysteria at the time.

"What are you looking for?" Michelle finally asked when Gator checked the stairs again with his flashlight. "Is the water getting higher?" It had already crept to the second stair.

"Rising water isn't the only thing we have to worry about," he said dully, snapping off the light.

"Then what?"

"He's looking for snakes," Reba said matter-of-factly. "Where there's water, there's snakes."

Michelle swallowed. "Snakes?"

Gator nodded. "Cottonmouths."

Michelle could almost taste the fear in her own mouth. She shuddered, and then scooted closer to her grandmother, trying to shut out the images around her. Somehow she would get through all this, she promised herself, and tomorrow, or at least soon, she'd have someone pull that tree off her car so she could return home. If only the wind and rain would stop. If only the water would go down and take the snakes with it. If only Gator hadn't kissed her and brought back all those disturbing feelings.

When the wind finally died down again to a steady whine, Gator insisted they try to rest, since none of them would be going anywhere until morning. After closing the bedroom door and stuffing clothes beneath it to prevent snakes from entering, Gator positioned himself in an old overstuffed chair while Reba and Michelle shared the antique iron bed and its feather mattress. Michelle was certain she'd never fall asleep, but somehow exhaustion forced her eyes closed. She opened them briefly when she heard Gator scuttling about the room with his flashlight, shining it on the floor and under the bed. But she was too tired to question him. Of course, had she known he was still looking for snakes ...

#

Morning came, and with it a beautiful blue sky. Michelle felt her heart soar at the sight of it, and she threw her arms around her grandmother, who gazed out the window beside her, looking very forlorn at the devastation around them.

"We're alive, Grand," Michelle whispered to the distraught woman. "Right now that's all that matters."

Gator, wearing another night's growth of beard, offered her a slight smile, and she thought he had never looked sexier. Not that it mattered, she reminded herself. The sooner she got away from Gator and the bayou, the better.

They crept down the stairs cautiously with Gator shining the flashlight in front of them. Although the water had gone down a bit, the first floor was soggy and full of mud. Gator turned to Reba.

"You can't stay here now. You know that, right?" The old woman refused to meet his gaze. "There's no electricity, and everything down here is wet and needs drying out. I'll try to find my boat, and if it's still in one piece, we'll use it to get out." When she didn't respond he went on. "We can take the hound and her puppies ... but the cats will have to stay. You can put food and water out, and they'll be fine for a couple of days."

"I can't leave Mister Ed," Reba said. "If there are snakes ... well, they'd go right for him, you know."

At the sound of his name, Mister Ed squawked loudly. Gator sighed and shook his head. "Just let me see if I can find the boat first. We'll tackle the other problems when we get to them."

"Where will we go?" Michelle asked.

"There are several shelters in town, but I'm certain they won't allow pets." He paused. "You're welcome to stay at my place—if it's still standing," he said. "At least until the two of you make arrangements." He made his way to the back door, wrenched it open, and glanced out. All at once he laughed.

"What is it?" Michelle hurried over and peered out the door. Gator's boat had somehow come through a screen, and part of it rested on the back porch, which was ankle-deep in water. The propeller had been torn off the motor and was nowhere in sight. One oar floated nearby and Gator grabbed it, knowing it was their only link to civilization.

"Wonder how long it's going to take me to paddle the three of us ten miles up the bayou," he said, his look amused, despite the arduous task that lay ahead.

Before Michelle knew what was happening, they were both laughing, great hearty chuckles that brought tears to her eyes. Reba joined them, laughing so hard she got a stitch in her side. The land around them lay in waste, but for the moment they couldn't get past the joy of being alive and unharmed.

By the time Gator and Michelle managed to get

the boat off the back porch, Reba had seen to the care of her cats and had boxed what supplies they might need for the trip. They located the other oar floating in the backyard near a shed. The hound and her puppies were loaded into the center of the boat where Reba was to sit, while Michelle sat in the front holding Mister Ed and his cage and feeling ridiculous. Gator shoved off from the back porch and began rowing.

The bayou had changed considerably with the deluge of water, but it presented no problem for Gator, who knew the area like his own bedroom. They rowed while the first reports came in on the radio. New Orleans and the barrier islands it seemed, had received the brunt of the storm; almost a hundred thousand people were without power and thousands were homeless, but it had not been as devastating as Katrina and the levies that protected the city had held.

At first Michelle was too engrossed in the sights around them to do anything more than stare. Here and there a warbler cried out, the first signs of life stirring after the storm. A bullfrog croaked from somewhere in the distance, and they caught sight of a white-tailed deer standing in the brush and mud looking at them in a dazed fashion. Still holding the birdcage in her arms, Michelle dozed. She awoke to the sound of a steady hum and glanced up as a small helicopter flew overhead. All three waved as the chopper dipped and circled over them, and then headed in another direction.

"They'll send somebody after us," Gator said, giving Reba a reassuring smile.

He was proved right. Within the hour a large boat rounded a bend of cypress trees. It was a welcome sight to the weary group.

Chapter Three

Once they'd been towed to the main pier, where Gator's newer-model pickup truck was parked, Michelle climbed into the back with the birdcage and dogs, feeling self-conscious and very much as if they were Louisiana's version of The Beverly Hillbillies. Gator immediately drove to the nearest shelter, which had been set up in City Hall. He parked his truck under a live oak so the animals would stay cool while they went inside. The mayor looked relieved to see Gator.

"We've been searching high and low for you, boy," he said, his cigar sending out puffy smoke rings over his head, as he completely ignored the NO SMOKING signs along the walls. "I was beginning to think something had happened to you."

Gator briefly explained the situation, but was more concerned about how the small town had fared during the storm. While he and the mayor held a short meeting, Reba and Michelle grabbed a cup of coffee. Sleeping bags littered the floor, several of them holding sleeping babies. Here and there groups of children played with toys while their parents stood nearby. Some were distraught over the situation, others seemed relieved to have it all behind them.

When Gator returned, looking tired and concerned, Michelle handed him her cup of coffee and he gladly accepted it. "One of our volunteer firemen has offered to drive you and the animals out to my place," he said. "He checked earlier and found it still standing. You're welcome to stay there, but I don't have time to take you myself right now." He glanced around. "As you can see, this place is a bit crowded, as I imagine the other shelters are. The motel down the street is full as well."

Michelle pondered the thought. The last place in the world she wanted to stay was with Gator Landry, but she didn't want to argue the point at the moment with so many other problems to attend to. Besides, they had to do something with Reba's pets.

Michelle hated to ask the question: Were there any deaths?"

Gator shook his head. "None in our town that I'm aware of. I can't answer for other areas. Quite a few injured folks, though, which is understandable. The nearest hospital is thirty miles away so there is a long line at our local clinic."

"Can you drive me there?" Michelle asked. "They may need an extra pair of hands."

He looked surprised. "Yeah, sure."

"I'll ride out to your place and see to my animals," Reba said. "But if it is okay with you, I'd just as soon come back here. Several of the couples need baby-sitters so they can drive out and check the damage to their homes."

Gator nodded, already moving to the back of the building, with another man in tow. The women followed. Reba's pets were quickly transferred to another vehicle. Michelle hugged her grandmother, and then climbed into Gator's truck.

The town had been hit hard, Michelle noted on the drive to the clinic. Power lines were down everywhere. Trees had been toppled, rooftops sheered from houses, metal signs bent or completely torn away. They passed a car that had been turned upside down, its wheels pointing to the sun, looking like a dead insect. The water had not yet receded significantly, but it hadn't stopped the workers, who wore knee-high rubber boots to get around.

"When do you think the telephone lines will be working?" Michelle asked Gator as he turned onto the main road. There was no cell phone reception because the local cell phone tower had been snapped in half by the storm.

"Hard to tell. We have emergency communications in place with a two-way radio channel back up system we dusted off. Is there someone you need to call?" He glanced at her. Of course there was, he told himself. Any woman with her looks would have a man waiting somewhere. "A boyfriend, perhaps?" he asked, knowing he wasn't being very subtle in his attempt to find out about her personal life.

Michelle met his questioning gaze. "That's kind of personal, isn't it?" she said.

Gator tightened his grip on the steering wheel. "Is that a yes or a no?" he finally asked.

Michelle, caught up in the sights around her, shot him a blank look. "What did you say?"

Gator sighed. "I'm trying to find out if you have a boyfriend, okay?"

"Why?"

"Just curious, that's all."

"I've had my share of boyfriends, yes," she said, wondering if he had picked up on the fact that she was speaking in the past tense. "What do you think I've been doing these sixteen years, sitting in some convent waiting for you to call? You never did call me, you know. Nor did you bother to write." There, she'd finally said it. But she was about sixteen years too late, she reminded herself.

He looked surprised. "You never gave me your address or telephone number."

"You could have gotten it easily enough from Reba."

Gator didn't answer right away. "I really didn't think you wanted me to contact you, Mic. After ... that night. You took off like a bat out of hell."

"I was scared."

"Of me?"

"Things were getting out of hand," she said. "If I had stayed, we probably would have ... well, you know."

"Would that have been so bad?"

She swung her head around so that she was looking at him once again. "I was sixteen years old, for Pete's sake! Of course it would have been bad." She sighed. "I shouldn't have sneaked out with you that night. I was just asking for trouble."

"Why did you?"

"Because I'd never really done anything that daring before. And it had sounded so romantic when you suggested it. I was naive. I'm not so naive anymore."

Gator felt silly for questioning her. He'd been crazy to think she would be even remotely interested in him after all this time. Of course there would have been other men in her life, and maybe there was somebody special now. He knew she wasn't married because Reba complained about it whenever he inquired about her, bemoaning the fact she would never have great-grandchildren. But kissing Michelle had brought back all those sweet memories of how she'd tasted and felt in his arms so long ago. He could only imagine what it would be like to make love to her. It was a bit late to think about those things now, he told himself. "I'll arrange for you to call your boyfriend this afternoon, Mic," he said softly, his voice resigned.

"I can't call him," she said matter-of-factly as Gator pulled into the parking lot of a large clinic. "His wife might object." She wasn't sure what had made her say it, other than the trace of bitterness left inside her over the breakup that had taken place six months earlier. She wasn't proud of her rancor; she had always been the type to forgive easily, but it still hurt from time to time.

Gator didn't respond right away. He parked his truck and turned off the engine. For a moment, he merely gazed at her, studying her profile. She was still about as pretty as they came, he decided. Her skin was flawless except for her nose, which was peppered with light freckles. She met his gaze. Her green eyes were cautious. "I'm sorry, Mic," he said at last.

Michelle arched her brows in surprise. "Sorry?" It wasn't exactly the response she'd expected.

He nodded. "I'm sorry you're involved in something like that."

"I'm not involved anymore," she told him. "I broke it off because he cheated." She paused. "The woman meant nothing to him, but when she became pregnant he ... Jeffrey ... did the honorable thing and married her. We're still friends, of course, since we have to work together. I guess I feel sorry for myself now and then, but I have a real problem with that sort of behavior." She stiffened when she caught him smiling. "What's so funny?"

"I just thought it odd that you don't kiss like a woman who's pining away over another man." Gator knew he wasn't being very sensitive, but he couldn't help himself. He didn't want to hear about the man in her life so why the hell had he asked? Maybe he had double standards; Lord knew he'd had his share of women these sixteen years.

Michelle felt the color drain from her face. He was, of course, talking about the kiss they'd shared during the eye of the storm. How like Gator to bring it up now, throw it in her face when she'd just confessed something very personal. "That didn't mean anything. I was afraid of dying. I was looking for anything to take my mind off the danger we were in."

Gator's jaw hardened perceptibly. The thought that she might have simply used him because the man she truly cared for was taken, irked him more than he wanted to admit. "Who are you trying to convince, Mic? Me or yourself?"

She wrenched the door open. He was making fun of her. He'd seen how terrified she had been. She had asked him to kiss her and had let him hold her close afterward because it felt as though the entire world had gone mad. Well, let him mock her. "You can be a real bastard when you put your mind to it, Gator Landry," she said. "I'd sooner drown myself in the bayou than get mixed up with the likes of you."

Gator winced at her words, but he knew he deserved it, even if he had been joking. Nevertheless, it was encouraging to know he could still rattle her. "Jeeze, Mic, when did you become so prickly?" He didn't wait for her to answer. "You were such a sweet, shy thing when we met. Now you're stuck on a married man and hurling insults at me. Next thing I know you'll be scribbling four-letter words on the bathroom walls."

Michelle climbed out of the truck and slammed the door. "I'm not sixteen years old anymore," she said through the open window. "I've seen the real world. I've worked with victims of drug overdoses, suicides, drive-by shootings and gang bangs. I've seen women beaten beyond recognition and—" She paused and shook her head as though to clear her mind. Why was she telling him all this? "You're the last person in the world to judge me, Gator Landry. You're unfit to call yourself sheriff of this town. Not only that—"

"There's no need to go on," he said, his eyes bright with humor. "I think you've established your feelings toward me." He started his engine. "But right now I have to get back to my duties. I may be a lousy sheriff, but I'm all these people have at the moment." He put the truck into gear and drove away, leaving Michelle standing in the parking lot feeling foolish. She'd always said and done foolish things when Gator was around. She would have thought she'd have grown out of it by now.

#

The staff at the clinic seemed relieved to have her there. One of the nurses found her a clean change of clothes, handed her a bucket of water, and showed her where she could wash up. The clinic, just like City Hall, had a backup generator, which meant there were lights. The storm had taught her a new appreciation for the simple luxuries, she thought as she emerged from the washroom fifteen minutes later feeling refreshed, her long hair combed and tied back at her neck.

Thankfully, there had been no deaths, although some of the people from the mobile-home park had been injured severely enough to be sent on to the hospital. An elderly man was brought in that afternoon with head injuries and a fractured leg. He'd been trapped under a collapsed building all night, and his condition was critical. While the doctor and his nurse stabilized him, Michelle assisted by applying a temporary leg splint. Once his vital signs improved, he was put into an ambulance and driven to the hospital. The staff spent the remainder of the day treating minor injuries, fractures, and strained backs.

When Gator arrived back at the clinic at the end of the day, he found Michelle in the lounge eating a hot dog, drinking coffee, and looking as tired as he felt. A couple of the restaurant owners in town had donated food that would have gone bad with no refrigeration. She offered him one of the hot dogs, and he accepted it, suddenly realizing he hadn't eaten all day. It had been one of the most grueling days of his life, searching through rubble for bodies. He'd found none, for which he was grateful. He'd deputized the volunteer members of the fire department, since there were no serious fires, and placed the men in town strategically to prevent looting.

"Do you need to hang around here?" Gator asked. "You look as though you could use a rest."

She nodded. "I am tired. The reception room has been packed all day, but I think everything is under control now."

"Why don't we drop by City Hall, pick up Reba, and go to my place," he suggested. "I think we deserve a break after what we've been through."

"That would be nice." She wadded up her hot dog wrapper and tossed it in a nearby trash can. She still didn't relish the thought of staying at Gator's, especially after their argument earlier, but at the moment she didn't seem to have much choice. "Just let me clear it with the others," she said, hurrying out of the room.

Ten minutes later they were on their way to City Hall. Neither of them spoke, and Michelle wondered if Gator felt as uncomfortable as she did. She decided she had better clear the air if she was going to be spending the night at his place.

"Look, I'm sorry about what I said earlier," she sputtered without preamble. She saw Gator's look of surprise and went on. "I don't know why I got so bent out of shape. Stress, I guess. This whole thing has turned me upside down."

Gator shrugged. "I had it coming. Sometimes I don't know when to stop pushing."

"I'd like the two of us to be friends," she said, "since it looks as though we're going to be spending the next couple of days together." She glanced away. "There's no reason to harbor bad feelings over something that happened sixteen years ago."

Gator knew that she was right, that they should put their differences aside. And he <u>had</u> been holding a grudge all these years, he realized. When she'd run away from him that night, he suspected he had pushed her too hard. Or maybe she'd had second thoughts and figured him for some kind of yokel or redneck. She was a big-city girl, straight out of Baton Rouge, where, he'd been certain, the guys his age were more sophisticated. Besides, he was only eighteen years old, and, although he was taking a couple of classes at the community college, he had no idea what he was going to do with his life. What could he have offered her?

Gator forced his thoughts back to the present. Michelle was looking at him, waiting for an answer. She wanted to be friends. How could a man be friends with the girl he'd first loved? Well, he would try anything once. "Sure, I'll be your friend," he said, breaking for a stop sign. "Why not?" It was crazy to expect more from a woman who was carrying a torch for another man.

Michelle smiled. "Good, let's shake on it." She offered her hand.

Taking her hand in his was his first mistake. Gator realized the minute his fist closed over hers. He almost jumped, and felt as if two raw wires had just made contact. The effect was immediate, sending powerful currents up his arms, and he was certain the hair along his forearm was standing on end. He released her, but he could still feel the small imprint of her hand in his palm. He gripped the steering wheel tightly and drove on, but he could not take his mind off how it had felt to hold that dainty hand, or how that hand would feel on his body in a loving caress. It was clear to him he could not touch her without wanting her.

Michelle would have had to be blind not to notice

the change in Gator. She, too, was shaken. How could an innocent handshake have such a powerful effect on her? This had nothing to do with mere friendship, she decided. His hand closing over hers had conveyed much more. She could imagine those leather-roughened hands on her skin. Those hands could yield strength and power or stroke a woman with a touch as light as dandelion fluff. The knowledge only heightened her awareness of him, and she wondered if there was a woman alive who was not susceptible to the very maleness of him.

#

Michelle returned to the shelter with Gator, but before they picked up Reba, she helped administer to several people with minor injuries. Gator watched, mesmerized. He could see the caring on her face and in the tender way he touched people. He could not help but develop a new respect for her.

It was late when Gator drove Michelle and Reba to his place, which turned out to be a blue, forty-foot-long houseboat located in a cove on the bayou. Surprisingly enough, it had sustained very little damage from the storm, except for a shattered window and some water leakage. His power was out, but that was the norm.

Using his flashlight to guide them, Gator helped Reba and Michelle out of the truck and led them onto the deck of the houseboat. He stopped at the door long enough to unlock it, then shined the light in so they could pass through first. “Watch your step,” he cautioned. “Just stay where you are till I find my kerosene lamp.”

As soon as they had light, Reba checked her hound and accepted Gator’s offer to take the dog out. Mister Ed began to squawk at the sight of them, but was quickly calmed by Reba’s voice. She draped a towel over his cage, and he went to sleep.

Michelle found herself standing in a living room of sorts, which was separated from a small kitchen by a counter. The living room furniture consisted of two sofa beds across from which stood a built-in bookcase holding a flat screen and stereo. The bookcase was filled with paperbacks and record albums, but it was too dark to see the titles. She held the lamp up to the entrance of a short hallway and found a small bedroom with an attached bath. Everything was surprisingly neat.

Reba yawned and stretched. “I’m so tired I could drop right here on the floor and it wouldn’t matter.” Michelle nodded, just as Gator came through the door with the dog.

“I found a couple of flashlights behind the seat in my truck,” he said, testing them to make sure they worked. He handed each of them one. “Maybe they’ll keep you from bumping into walls. You two can have the bed, and I’ll take the couch,” Gator said. “But first”—he paused and glanced at Reba, his look amused—"I'd better change the sheets."

Reba merely chuckled, but Michelle rolled her eyes heavenward. "We'd appreciate it very much," she said, sarcasm ringing loud in her voice. Heaven only knew what kind of unnatural acts he'd performed on those sheets.

In the end, Michelle helped him change them, all the while refusing to meet his gaze, which she knew was bright with silent laughter. The man was totally without scruples, she decided. She was thankful it was dark and he couldn't see the bright blush on her cheeks.

"Would you like to wash up?" Gator asked as soon as they'd finished making the bed. "I have several jugs of water in the back of my truck. And I always keep a couple of toothbrushes on hand in case I have company."

"Yes, I'll just bet you do," Michelle replied.

Her words seemed to amuse him even more. "Just let me find you and Reba something to wear, and then I'll get the water."

Once Reba had washed up and changed into fresh clothes, Michelle poured water into the bathroom sink and bathed her face and the back of her neck, then washed as best she could. Gator had given them both a toothbrush, and Michelle took great delight in brushing her teeth for the first time in two days. Maybe she was being too hard on the man, she decided. He was going out of his way to make them comfortable, and it was none of her business what he did with his personal life. He'd worked tirelessly throughout the day to get the town back on its feet, despite the fact that he'd never wanted the job. She had to give him credit for that.

For her, helping others had been a conscious act of meeting her own needs. With her parents so heavily involved in their medical-supply business, which took them all over the country, she'd spent a lot of time with baby-sitters and nannies. And without brothers and sisters, there was a certain amount of loneliness involved. She'd admired her parents' business skills, but she'd been more impressed with the doctors and nurses she met through their dealings and the gentle one-on-one relationships that existed between the medical professionals and their patients.

Her parents had suggested medical school, which they were certainly able to afford, but she had not been interested in becoming a doctor, who was, in her opinion, a mere figurehead of the medical profession. It was the nurses who made the difference, she decided. They were the ones who did all the hand-holding, who soothed patients' fears and reassured them in the middle of the night. By becoming a nurse, she had fulfilled both other people's needs and her own.

It was only later that Michelle realized it wasn't

enough. Jeffrey Rigby was fresh out of medical school, ready to conquer the world. He wasn't hardened like the older doctors—he genuinely cared about his patients. Michelle had caught him crying in the supply room once after losing a young boy he had tried to revive. It had drawn them closer together. So close, in fact, that he often turned to her with his problems. She was only too glad to be there for him. He gave so much of himself that it was only fitting she console him and be his anchor of support when things got tough. And when he'd kissed her one morning after a particularly grueling night in emergency, the bond had grown stronger.

This was love, she decided. It didn't matter that there weren't fireworks or bells going off in her head. It was two human beings connecting. It did not matter that their lovemaking was not the stuff that made up erotic romance literature. It was gentle and pleasurable, like a soothing balm to a weary soul. And when he'd confessed his brief fling with the nurse in radiology, she'd tried to forgive him. When he'd told her about the baby and his decision to marry the woman, she'd had no choice but to break off their relationship. Still, she'd remained his friend. The pain in his eyes was proof that he'd suffered enough. She'd had to put away the hurt and concentrate on being strong, his "tower of strength," as he often called her. There would be no more intimacy, she told him, because her sense of right and wrong would not allow it. But she would always be there for him to talk to.

In the beginning it had been difficult. She had dreamed of a future with him. They had common interests and goals, and they both wanted children one day. Now another woman would carry those children. It wasn't fair, Michelle told herself, when she passed the woman in the nurses' lounge or hallway, watching her waistline thicken with each passing month. She had not realized until then how much she longed for a child, to have the family she'd never had growing up. But it was not to be. Thankfully, the pain had eased over the ensuing months, but not the feeling of rejection and betrayal. She would not make the same mistake again.

When Michelle finally came out of the bathroom, she found Reba already in bed, fast asleep. She changed into the cotton shirt Gator had given her and laughed at the size of it. The hem almost reached her knees, and the sleeves were at least six inches too long. She rolled them up to her elbows. Gator tapped lightly on the bedroom door and she opened it.

"You finished with the toothpaste?" he said.

"Oh, sorry. I'll get it for you." Michelle retrieved it from the bathroom and carried it into the kitchen, where Gator was washing up at the sink. He'd stripped off his shirt and was in the process of soaping his chest, stomach, and underarms. Michelle was riveted to the spot, unable to pry her gaze from him. His jeans rode low on his hips in a way that made her eyes dilate. No matter what she thought of him personally, he was undoubtedly one of the finest-looking men she'd ever laid eyes on. She knew men, Jeffrey included, who spent hours at the gym but didn't come close to looking so good. She wondered if Gator worked out, but she didn't think so. She could imagine him chopping wood or swimming in the river to stay in shape, but she couldn't envision him lifting weights or running an asphalt track in expensive sweats.

"Would you pass me that towel?" Gator asked, leaning over the sink as he rinsed the soapy foam from his body with a washcloth. It was one of the most sensual acts she'd ever seen.

Michelle reached for the towel on the counter and handed it to him. He dried himself briskly, then draped the towel around his neck. "Are you hungry?"

Michelle shook her head. It was all she could do to keep her eyes off his chest, the way the blue-black curls glistened in the lamplight, the way his nipples beaded in the cool night air. "I'm too tired to eat," she finally said. But mostly she was tense, all wound up, no doubt from all the coffee she'd drank that evening—and from spending so much time with him, she thought.

"Which is a good thing since all I have is beer and pretzels. You don't impress me as a beer drinker." Gator had never been much of a beer drinker himself until he'd worked in the sugar cane fields. It had become a habit to share a cold beer with the rest of the men at the end of a long, hot day. He couldn't drink like most men; it was his metabolism, he supposed. Three beers wouldn't get him drunk but would certainly give him one hell of a headache the following day. The guys at the Night Life Lounge teased him unmercifully about it, and got a kick out of it when, after a couple of brews, he ordered diet soda.

"Right now anything sounds good," Michelle said. She hoped the beer would relax her. Although she was exhausted, she was not ready to climb into bed with her grandmother, whom she knew snored louder than a jumbo jetliner.

Gator reached into the small refrigerator and pulled out two beers. "They're still cool," he said, putting one metal can to his forehead. He popped the metal top on one and handed it to her, then reached inside a cabinet for the pretzels.

Michelle took a seat at the counter and sipped her beer slowly, gazing across at Gator in the dimly lit room. The flame from the lamp painted shadows across his dark face. He leaned on the counter, his elbows propped beneath him, his chin anchored on one fist.

"After watching you tonight, I see why you decided to become a nurse," he said. "You have a calming effect on people." Except on him, he thought. Every nerve in his body came alive when she was near. "I suppose it's a bit dull working in this place after the excitement of working in a big city hospital."

"Not dull, just different. I'm probably more sympathetic to these people, because they can't help what happened to them. Many of the people I work with at my emergency room are responsible in some way for their own injuries or deaths."

"Oh, we have our share of problems here," Gator said. "Domestic violence, drunk drivers, fights."

"Is that why you decided to become sheriff?" She knew it wasn't, but for some reason she wanted to hear it from him.

He straightened and folded his arms over his chest. "I became sheriff because I was elected. I've never had any grand illusions about trying to change the world. I don't really care what goes on around me as long as it doesn't interfere with my life. To someone like you, that probably sounds selfish, but that's the way I am. What you see is what you get."

"Why do you think you were elected in the first place?"

"Because my father was sheriff for so long. Folks just expected me to take over where he left off, I suppose."

"I understand the people thought a great deal of him."

"Yes, and they never fail to remind me how great he was. And now that he's dead it's like he's a national hero or something. You can't compete with somebody like that. But I have more important plans for my life than playing *Andy of Mayberry*, and the sooner I find somebody to take my place, the better off we'll all be."

She nodded. "Do you plan to live here for a while?" she asked, glancing around.

"I'm considering my options. I try not to stray too far because I need to be able to check in with my mom from time to time, see that she has what she needs and is okay."

"I know what that's like," Michelle said. "I constantly worry about my grandmother, but after this experience I'm going to have a phone installed, even if I have to personally meet with someone from the phone company. Then I'm going to insist she wear one of those necklaces or bracelets from a monitoring company in case she has an accident."

Gator smiled. "Something tells me she isn't going to like it."

"I'm not giving her a choice in the matter."

"Sounds like a case of tough love."

"Yup. I'm too much of a softie, but after what we just went through I'm going to insist on changes."

Michelle checked her wristwatch. "I need to head to bed. Will you be comfortable out here?"

"I'm good."

She stood and placed her empty beer can beside the sink. "By the way, I don't suppose you have any idea when I can get someone to pull that tree off my car." She hadn't wanted to bother him with it earlier, since he'd been so busy.

Gator regarded her, a half-smile playing on his lips. He wondered if she knew how sexy she looked in his shirt, with her hair hanging loose. "You in a hurry to get back to Baton Rouge, Mic?" he asked.

"Well I do have a job there, you know."

He nodded thoughtfully. "You're sure it doesn't have something to do with your old boyfriend?"

The question surprised her. "Of course not. He has a wife."

Gator stood, and the little kitchen area grew even smaller in size. He gazed down at Michelle thoughtfully. Without thinking, he reached for a curl and rubbed it between his fingers. "If you and I were sharing the same bed, there wouldn't be another woman carrying my baby." He raised the curl to his mouth and brushed it across his full bottom lip. "I like to keep my sleeping arrangements simple. That way nobody gets shot."

He knew he was totally out of line for saying such a thing, but jealousy was eating at his gut and he couldn't help it. He had no claim on her, but the mere thought of her loving another man made him crazy. He had thought of her over the years, but the pictures he'd conjured in his mind—her leaning over a sick patient or lunching with the other nurses in the hospital cafeteria—had never included another man. It wasn't what he truly believed, he realized now. He'd simply been fooling himself.

Michelle didn't know what to say at first. His words had caught her off guard. She could only gaze at his eyes, which looked like glittering onyx in the dim light. Her heart was pounding so loud, she was afraid he could hear it. She pulled her hair from his grasp. "Are you trying to tell me you're a one-woman man, Gator?" she asked once her senses had returned. She didn't give him a chance to respond. "Because if you are, let me assure you I don't believe it. You with that ... that hickey on your neck."

He grinned. "It's not a hickey, Mic."

"Yeah, right." Her voice was edged with sarcasm.

This time he chuckled softly. "It's a bee sting, darlin'. I had an allergic reaction. But don't get me wrong; I'm not opposed to having a woman give me a love bite. I just prefer they do it where it doesn't show. No sense advertising what I do in bed. Know what I mean?"

She didn't know whether to believe him or not. "You led me to believe the worst."

"I did it because I love to see you get riled. Just like I let you believe I'd had some woman tangled up in my sheets and had to pull them off the bed before you caught something. I didn't want to ruin your bad impression of me by letting you think I was only trying to be a good host. You see, my mama taught me a long time ago that I should have clean sheets and towels when company came; as well as a new toothbrush. But it was more fun watching your imagination run away with you."

"You did it because you enjoy laughing at me."

His look sobered. "I'd never laugh at you, Mic."

Michelle swallowed. She wondered if she would ever be able to hold a conversation with him without her emotions running the full gamut. One minute he was teasing her, the next he was charming her socks off, and at a moment's notice he would turn thoughtful and sincere. The man was full of contradictions. She couldn't keep up with him. Perhaps that's how he operated—he confused the woman, then made his move. She pitied the poor woman who got involved with him. A relationship with Gator would be stormy and unbalanced, filled with peaks and valleys, never smooth running.

"I have to go to bed now," she said, feeling the need to put some distance between them. She felt vulnerable with him, and it made her uncomfortable. Although he held up his end of the conversation as well as the next person, she was constantly aware that just below that thin line of conventionality, there was a very potent man who exuded raw masculinity and knew precisely what buttons to push when dealing with a female. She missed the easygoing, uncomplicated relationship she'd had with Jeffrey.

"G'night, Mic," he said softly.

Michelle turned for the bedroom, but she could feel his gaze on her. She didn't feel safe until she was inside the room with the door closed behind her. But sleep was a long time coming. Every time she closed her eyes, she saw Gator's face. He was dangerous, she told herself. He had promised to protect her from the storm, but who was going to protect her from him and these feelings she had every time he was near?

Chapter Four

The Red Cross arrived two days later with tents and donated items, most of which were used for those families who'd lived in the mobile-home park that had been virtually destroyed. Water bottles and ice and various other food supplies began coming in on trucks, so that people's immediate needs were met. Gator and the town's other officials had combed the area, sifting through debris, while Michelle had divided her time between the clinic and shelters. Gator had also checked on Reba's cats, putting out bags of food and fresh water and performing what he called the "god-awful task" of changing their kitty litter. Although the water had gone down somewhat, he cautioned Reba about returning too soon.

When Michelle was finally able to get through on a landline phone to the hospital, she found her co-workers frantic, but more than understanding that she could not return right away, especially when her car was still buried under a tree. The hospital was understaffed since they'd sent medical personnel to New Orleans, and when Michelle spoke with Jeffrey, she learned he'd been pulling double shifts right along with everyone else. He sounded exhausted and a bit irritated that she hadn't called sooner.

"We've tried to find out about you several times, Michelle," he said. "All they told us was there had been no casualties. Nobody knew if you were injured, and you didn't tell any of us your grandmother's name."

"I'm sorry, Jeffrey," she said, feeling guilty for making everyone worry so. Heaven knew Jeffrey had enough to deal with at the moment, what with a new wife who was pregnant. "The cell phone tower was down and what little bandwidth there was made personal calls a luxury this town couldn't afford. And in the beginning I was more concerned with taking care of the emergencies. This landline phone has only been working since this morning, and the whole town is using it." She paused. "You sound dead on your feet."

"I am. I've been sleeping at the hospital every night, and you know what that's like. But it beats the heck out of going home. It's not working out, Michelle. I made a mistake. I don't know how long I can take it."

She was genuinely sorry for him. The man had

tried to do the right thing by marrying the woman, and she knew he was paying emotionally. "Just hang in there, Jeffrey," she said. "I'll be home in a couple of days and we'll talk."

"What kind of life is this, Michelle?" he said, sounding on the verge of tears. "All I do is work. My patients don't appreciate me—they want more. They're takers, Michelle. And then I have to go home to a wife who does not like me and is sick all the time. There's no payoff, no joy in my existence. I can't take much more."

Michelle was growing irritated with his whining. "Don't talk like that, Jeffrey," she said firmly, wondering when he'd first started acting like a cry baby. He was a grown man—a doctor, for heaven's sake! Perhaps his work in the emergency room was taking its toll. "You're stronger than you think. This has been a bad time for you, but you'll get through it." She glanced over her shoulder to where a group of people had congregated at the door, each of them anxious to use the landline telephone. "Look, Jeffrey, I have to get off. People are waiting to use the phone."

"When are you coming home?"

"As soon as I can. I promise. Good-bye, Jeffrey." She hung up the telephone, shaking her head, wondering if life would ever return to normal.

"Everything okay?" Gator asked, noting the worried expression on her face.

Michelle didn't speak until she was out of hearing distance from the others. "I need to go home, Gator," she said as soon as he'd joined her.

"Let the guy work out his own problems, Mic."

"I don't expect you to understand."

"I understand a man has to take responsibility for his own actions. Stand on his own two feet. You're not his mother."

She didn't appreciate him sticking his nose in her business. "I happen to be his friend."

"His problems are between him and his wife. Besides, he had his chance with you and blew it."

Her anger flared. "You have no right to pry into my personal life, and you certainly have no right to pass judgment on a man like Jeffrey. What do you know about honor and obligation? You can't wait to dump your own responsibilities into somebody else's lap and go on with your life. Jeffrey doesn't have that freedom."

"So are you thinking maybe the woman tricked him?"

Michelle blinked several times. "I never said that."

"Maybe not in so many words, but you keep putting him in the victim's role."

"Let's just drop it, okay," she said, feeling a bit emotional over the whole thing. Gator had a way of making it all sound even worse, cheap and tawdry were two words that came to mind. She wondered why Gator was getting involved in the first place. She had come to terms with the broken relationship with Jeffrey a long time ago; in fact, there were times she wondered what she had even seen in Jeffrey. But Gator had no right to rub her nose in her mistakes.

"I'm not going to discuss this with you," she said, holding her hand up to halt the conversation. "But I really need to get back home. If you won't help me find someone to get that tree off my car, I'll do it myself. "

Gator realized now that he'd been too rough on her. Once again he'd let his emotions get the best of him. He wanted to apologize for hurting her feelings, kiss away the pain, but it wasn't the place. "The heavy equipment is needed elsewhere at the moment, Mic, you know that. And what are you going to do about your grandmother? Somebody has to help her get her place in order. She's too old to do it alone."

Michelle buried her face in her hands. She was so tired. She was tired of living on stale hot dogs and black coffee. She was tired of wearing the same clothes and of washing her bra and panties out every night in the bathroom sink. But she knew he spoke the truth; somebody had to help Reba. With her parents out of the country till the end of the month, she was the only one Reba had to rely on. But that was the story of her life. Her parents had never been around, not for her or anyone else.

Michelle dropped her hands to her side. “Can you take me out to Reba’s place tomorrow?” she asked. “I’d like to get started right away.”

“Okay, Mic. Lord knows, I wouldn’t want you to hang around any longer than necessary.” He gave a grunt of disgust and turned around to arrange his bedding. Jealousy, he decided, was truly the monster it was reported to be. He hoped for his sake this was his first and last brush with it.

#

Reba’s place was a disaster. Gator and Michelle arrived early the next morning in his boat. Although Reba’s house could be reached by car, the distance was much longer that way, and many of the back roads were still impossible to navigate without a chainsaw and bulldozer. Reba had lost two outbuildings, and the screens on her back porch flapped in the breeze like laundry on a clothesline. A number of windows had been shattered, and tree limbs and various other debris littered the yard, giving it a shabby, unkempt appearance that was alien to Reba’s way of life. Her boat dock and part of the backyard were still covered with water. For the most part, the water had subsided, but mud and debris was everywhere.

The inside of the house wasn’t much better, and Michelle was thankful that Gator had convinced

Reba to stay at his mother's house for a couple of days. The woman had not seemed to mind Reba's pets, and Michelle thought it was high time Reba reacquainted herself with old friends instead of keeping to herself as she had since the death of her husband.

"I don't know where to begin," Michelle said, taking in her surroundings. The large braided rug in the living room was soggy, as were the numerous throw rugs scattered across the plank floors. She faced Gator. "You don't need to be here," she said. "I appreciate it, but I know you have more important things to do in town." She didn't know how she would manage without his help, but she felt guilty for taking up so much of his time already.

"Don't worry about it, Mic. I've deputized half the town. They can spare me for a day or two."

"Why are you doing this?" she finally asked. Gator didn't seem the type to go out of his way for another human being unless he was motivated by guilt or obligation. He owed her nothing. Although he'd worked nonstop the past few days since the storm had hit, she knew that he really didn't want to be there, he was merely biding his time.

Gator shrugged. "It's the least I can do. The people in this town looked after my mother when I moved away. I'd come back to check on her from time to time and find someone had chopped wood or weeded her garden and flower beds for her. I reckon it wouldn't kill me to return the favor. "He pressed the toe of his boot against the large rug, and water streamed across the floor. "First thing we need to do is get this rug out of here so the floor can dry."

Michelle sensed he was eager to get started and didn't want to waste time arguing. For the next half hour, they concentrated on getting the rug outside, where they draped it across several old sawhorses to dry. Michelle wasn't sure the rug could be saved, but knowing that Reba never threw anything away, she was hesitant to do so herself.

Although it was still early, the day was hot and muggy. Gator, already drenched with perspiration, had shrugged out of his shirt and tied an old blue bandanna around his forehead. A fine sheen of sweat covered his back, shoulders, and chest, and tiny sweat beads glistened across his forehead and upper lip. That, combined with his unshaven face, convinced Michelle that he'd never looked more rakish or devilishly sexy.

A shave and shower these days would have been sheer luxury, she knew. Although Gator had conveniently disappeared each night during the bath rituals to give Reba and Michelle privacy, there was still something very intimate about sharing the same bar of soap, the same tube of toothpaste, the same sink. Gator often waited until the women were in bed before he began his own ablutions, and Michelle had raptly listened to the sounds he made—the water splashing against the metal sink, Gator humming under his breath as he washed. In her mind she saw him standing naked before the sink, the kerosene lamp painting shadows on his large, hair-roughened body.

Michelle forced her thoughts to the present as she followed Gator inside the house once more. They threw open the windows—those that hadn't been broken during the storm—to aid in drying out the place. Michelle began the enormous task of mopping while Gator measured the windows and cut plastic from a large roll he'd purchased from the hardware store that morning. He'd brought a staple gun to make the job easier, courtesy of FEMA. Michelle had only finished mopping half the living room floor when Gator called for help.

"I need you to hold these plastic sheets up while I staple them in place," he said, rolling the sheets up so they would be easier to handle. "Why don't we start upstairs so the bottom floors have longer to dry?" Michelle nodded and followed.

Gator had Michelle hold the plastic against the window while he stapled it to the frame securely. Michelle decided it was the most unnerving moment in her life having to stand there, stretched to her full height as she held the plastic in place, while he stood directly behind her and tacked it in. She could feel his breath on the back of her neck, sending delightful tingles down her spine. When his big chest brushed her shoulder blades accidentally, she sucked in her breath and tried to make herself smaller. She suddenly felt vulnerable dressed in shorts that were a tad tight and a cotton blouse that exposed her midriff every time she raised her arms. They'd seemed practical enough when she'd chosen them at the shelter; with clothing so scarce, she'd been lucky to find something close to her size. She decided after a moment that clothing had nothing to do with the way she felt. Gator Landry could make a woman in a nun's habit feel naked.

When Gator finally finished nailing the plastic in place, he dropped his arms to his side and backed away from the window. Michelle, who'd been literally holding her breath, exhaled with such force that it almost made her dizzy. She grasped the windowsill for support.

"You okay?" Gator asked, arching one brow quizzically.

"Yeah, fine."

"How come your face is so red?"

She fumbled for a reply. "It's the ... heat."

"I hope you're not pregnant too."

Michelle faced him. "Of course I'm not pregnant. What on earth would make you say such a thing?"

He shrugged. "I just thought it would be kind of funny if your good doctor knocked up his wife and mistress at the same time."

Her cheeks flamed. "I'm not his mistress."

"Call it what you like, Mic, but it all adds up to the same thing."

This time it took every ounce of willpower she had to keep from flying into a rage. "I am not sleeping with him!" she shouted. "Not that it's any of your damn business. I'm not sleeping with anyone! You got that, Sheriff Landry or do you have more personal and insulting remarks you'd like to toss my way?"

He really could be a jerk, he told himself. He tried to smooth it over with a bit of humor. "So that explains the bitchy behavior and those lines on your forehead, Miss Thurston. You obviously need some male attention, and it just so happens I can fit you into my schedule at the moment."

Michelle crossed her arms and shot him a dark look. "There you go again," she said. "Just when I'm beginning to think your morals have crept a bit higher than a snake's belly, you do your darnedest to prove me wrong."

He looked amused. "Wouldn't want to disappoint you."

"You could never do that, Sheriff, because my opinion of you was fairly low to begin with."

Gator stepped closer. "I seem to remember a time when it wasn't so low, Mic."

"I was sixteen and dumb. I was also bored and

had nothing better to do."

He smiled, remembering that night so many years ago. "I remember you lying in my arms on the sweet smelling grass with the night breeze playing in your hair."

"We were on your mother's quilt."

"Beneath a giant live oak."

"It was a magnolia tree."

The smile changed to a grin. "For somebody who was bored out of her mind, you certainty remember it well."

Michelle blushed. "I have an excellent memory. I never forget a thing."

"Remember what you whispered in my ear that night?"

She glanced away and swallowed. "No."

He tilted his head forward so that she was looking directly into his eyes. "You said I made you feel things you'd never felt before."

"Gator Landry, you're a liar! I never said such a thing."

He nodded slowly. "Oh, yes you did." He crooked a finger beneath her chin and raised her face. "We were both so hot that night, I thought we'd catch fire."

His voice was low but smooth, a liquid purr to her ears that made her mouth go dry and the back of her throat itch. Michelle could only gaze into the black eyes that held her so totally captivated. "I keep reminding you that was a long time ago," she finally said. "I don't think I actually realized what I was getting into until you pulled me down on that quilt. But now I'd just as soon forget it, if you don't mind."

He cocked his head to the side as though pondering her request. "I don't think we can forget it, Mic," he said honestly. How was he supposed to forget the way she'd felt that night when she insisted on cavorting around in those too-short shorts? And where had she found that blouse, for Pete's sake? Every time she took a breath the hem shimmied up her rib cage and he caught sight of peach-colored flesh. He'd almost lost it when he'd spied that kissable navel riding her waistband. He dropped his finger from her chin and rested his hand on her shoulder.

"I don't think we'll ever stop wondering what it would be like between us now, if only we could stop playing games with each other and face our feelings. If we were that volatile as teenagers, what do you think we'd be like as adults?"

Michelle backed away, wanting to escape the feel of his hand on her. But even as she broke physical contact with him, the impact of his touch lingered. His words had painted a picture in her mind that was much too dangerous to even contemplate. What he was suggesting was crude and indecent, as far as she was concerned. What about love or caring or all the other things that made up a relationship? She almost laughed out loud at the thought. Gator Landry had made it plain from the beginning that he didn't desire a relationship. He was merely looking for a bed partner to entertain him until he could move on. Well, he could look elsewhere, she told herself.

"Are the women in Temptation getting so scarce that you have to harass every woman who comes into town?" she asked.

"Not at all."

Michelle gritted her teeth at the smug look on his face. The man certainly had a high opinion of himself. "Then why don't you find somebody who's a bit more susceptible to your charms, instead of forcing yourself on someone who isn't?"

He grinned. "I like you, Mic. You've got style. I've always been partial to classy women. Just as long as they don't carry it too far into the bedroom."

Gator turned and reached for another sheet of plastic. He was purposely goading her, he knew, but he couldn't help himself. He enjoyed watching her get so flustered she couldn't think straight. She was fumbling for a comeback even now, and it delighted him that she was having trouble forming a reply. He was aware that his playful banter irritated the hell out of her, but he couldn't help himself. Part of it, he knew, was to get back at her, because she wanted to return home so badly. Although she claimed it was her job she was concerned about, he wondered just how much of it actually had to do with the man who'd once been her lover. It irked him that she had fallen for a doctor. But he could see her playing the demure doctor's wife, attending charity functions, raising yellow-haired kids with braces on their teeth. He gritted his own teeth at the thought.

Michelle didn't quite know how to respond to his comment, so she said nothing. To respond would merely keep their argument alive, and that, in her opinion, was a waste of time. Let Gator think what he wanted. She was there for one thing—to see after her grandmother. The sooner she finished, the sooner she'd be on the highway to Baton Rouge.

#

They worked nonstop the rest of the day, halting only briefly to eat the lunch Reba had prepared that morning.

It was still early when they packed the boat to head home, but Gator wanted to make sure they got in before dark. A man could get lost forever on the bayou at night, he knew.

The house was, for the most part, habitable, although the grounds were still in bad shape, despite all Gator had done. They decided to come back the following day and try to finish up so Reba wouldn't have to worry about it when she returned. While Gator loaded the boat, Michelle put out fresh food and water for the cats and changed the litter boxes. She was on her way out the back door when she spied Gator standing dead still, one arm rigidly extended toward the ground, his pistol aimed at something. She sucked her breath in sharply as she caught sight of his target, a large snake, poised and ready to strike, not more than ten feet from him. The gunshot was deafening, reverberating in the air as the snake fell to the ground in a macabre fashion.

"Is it ... dead?" Michelle asked breathlessly. Gator swung his head in her direction and saw the horrified look on her face. He walked over and kicked the snake with the toe of his boot. "Yeah, I'd say so." He picked it up by the tail. "He's fairly big. I'd say he was the granddaddy of the bunch."

"W-what kind of snake is it?" She realized suddenly that she was trembling.

"Cottonmouth. I'm surprised we didn't run into one sooner."

She glanced around anxiously, scanning the grass for others. "You think there are more around here?"

"It wouldn't surprise me." At her frightened look, he added, "But don't worry, they're just as scared of us as we are of them. Most of the time they'll run in the opposite direction if they hear you coming. I think I surprised this one." He slung the snake in the water and it landed with a plop, sending ripples in every direction. Michelle shuddered.

"Can we leave now?" she asked, determined to put as much distance as she could between herself and the possibility of more snakes. She was thankful now that Gator's mother had insisted she and Reba spend the night at her place, with its wide, fern-filled front porch and wicker rockers. It seemed a bit more civilized than Reba's home or Gator's houseboat. Not only that, Mrs. Landry had promised to fill her bathtub with warm water so Michelle could take a real bath when she returned. The prospect of that luxury had been on Michelle's mind all day.

"Sure, hop in," he said, motioning her over. He held the boat still while she climbed in. Once she'd settled herself in the bow, he cast the lines and started the motor. A minute later they were on their way. Michelle leaned back and closed her eyes, enjoying the light breeze on her face. It felt good to rest after a long day of hard work.

They hadn't gone more than a hundred feet from the dock before the motor started sputtering. They both glanced up in surprise, but before they could say anything, it died.

Michelle straightened in her seat. "What's wrong? Are we out of gas?"

Gator shook his head. "I just changed gas tanks." He shrugged. "It sounds like something is wrong with the gas, but it's been awhile since I've worked on boats."

"What are we going to do?"

Gator wasn't listening. He'd already moved to the back of the boat, testing hoses, looking into the red gas tank, sniffing it. Finally, he raised up. "I think there is water in the gas line."

"Is it serious?"

"No, but I'll have to clean the gas lines."

"How long will it take?"

"Shouldn't take more than an hour, but that's not our problem."

"Then what is our problem?" she asked, almost dreading his answer.

"We don't have any more gas. This was my last tank. It's full, but it won't do us a bit of good if it's got water in it."

"Can't you radio for help?"

"We're too far out."

"Well, don't worry, Reba and your mother will send someone out here for us," she said hopefully.

"I wouldn't count on it."

"Why?"

"Because folks don't like coming way out here on the bayou at night. For one thing, the bayou is always changing, especially after a storm. A person could get lost and never be found out here."

"Then they'll just have to take the road, for heaven's sake. I know it is much farther that way, but we could walk to the nearest—" She stopped speaking when Gator glanced away. “What’s wrong?”

Gator didn’t answer right away. “One of the bridges was washed out by the storm.” He heard her gasp and looked up. “I didn’t want to tell you, because I knew you’d get upset, what with your car still buried under that tree and all. I figured it would only be a couple of days before the bridge was fixed, and I didn’t want to bother you with it.”

“Oh, well, that’s just dandy,” she said, feeling her chest swell with anger. “You knew all this time and didn’t bother to tell me.”

“What good would it have done?”

“I could have ... maybe made arrangements to have someone drive down from Baton Rouge to get me. I just thought it was a matter of having a tree pulled from my car.”

“I hope you don’t expect the good doctor to leave his pregnant wife to come down and rescue you,” he said dryly.

Michelle could not believe he was still harping on Jeffrey. “What is wrong with you?” she demanded. “You’re obsessed with Jeffrey. I should never have told you about him.”

“He’s the reason you’re so anxious to get back.”

“No, he’s not!” she almost shouted. “I have a job I need to get back to. You might be able to toss your badge aside and walk away, but that’s not the way I do things. I take my responsibilities seriously.”

"I don't have to explain myself to you or anyone else," he said.

"That is exactly how I feel, but you constantly badger me about things that are none of your business. I'm sick of it. I'm sick of this whole mess, and I am damn sick of you meddling in my business. So back off! Just leave me the hell alone because I have reached my limit and can't take anymore, especially from you."

Gator reached for the oars.

"What are you doing?"

"I'm going to beat you with this paddle," he said matter-of-factly, "if you don't stop ranting and raving at me. While you've been throwing your temper tantrum, we've drifted farther from the house."

Michelle crossed her arms over her breasts and pressed her lips together in a firm line. She was too tired and angry to speak at the moment.

Twenty minutes later, Gator docked the boat at Reba's backyard once more. Michelle hadn't so much as uttered a word to him in that time, and she clambered out of the boat before he had a chance to put the oars away and assist. She stalked up to the house and slammed inside, wishing the bayou would open up and swallow Gator whole so that she never had to look at him again.

Chapter Five

Michelle busied herself inside for the next couple of hours, trying to make use of what light was left for the day. Gator came in once looking for rubbing alcohol, which he planned to use to flush out the fuel line. Once she found it for him, he thanked her abruptly and left. Her mood was so bleak; she decided it best not to say anything.

Gator glanced at the house from time to time as he worked, but Michelle hadn't budged from the place. He thought about walking to Reba's nearest neighbor, several miles away, but he knew he'd be wasting his time, since that very neighbor was probably still sitting in one of the shelters in town. Besides, he and Michelle were no worse off than the rest of the town at the moment.

Gator knew his mother would not grow concerned right away. He had told her they might drop by City Hall before returning, so she wouldn't expect them back anytime soon. He knew she had every confidence that he could find his way around the bayou, but then she had always trusted his judgment, even in his rebellious days when everything he did sent his father into a frenzy.

Gator frowned. His father had never given an inch. He had expected his son to be a man at ten years old, as he'd watched their house burn to the ground with everything in it—his Hardy Boys mysteries, video games, and all the treasures he'd accumulated in his short life. Even so, while his father had ruled with an iron fist, his mother had raised him with unconditional love. It was uncanny that the man was admired and respected by those he served, because Gator and his mom dreaded the end of the work day when he would pull into the driveway. Gator had decided long ago that if he ever had children, he would not hold back his affection.

But none of that was important right now, he reminded himself. Besides, it was unlikely that he would marry and have children at this point in his life, with all he wanted to see and do. What mattered to him at the moment was getting Michelle and himself back to town. He felt helpless. For someone who was accustomed to being in control, it was not a comfortable feeling. But the damn hurricane had fouled up everything!

Michelle had counted on him to get her back, and he'd let her down. She had every right to be angry. Her entire life was waiting for her back in

Baton Rouge, but she was spinning her wheels in the boonies simply because of him. He should have thought to bring another gas tank. He should have checked the progress on the bridge. He should have insisted someone pull that damn tree off her car. But he hadn't, simply because he hadn't wanted to see her go. Once again, he was proving to be a selfish bastard. He promised himself he would do something about it as soon as he reached town, even if he had to repair the bridge with his own bare hands, even if it meant driving Michelle back to Baton Rouge personally.

Michelle stood in the living room gazing out the window at Gator, who had not budged from his place in the boat for almost two hours. She could barely make him out in the diminishing light, but he looked deep in thought as he stared out at the water. What could he be thinking? Guilt stabbed her. She'd had no right to say the things she had to him, even if he had deserved it at times. She should have been more patient. After all, he'd done everything he could for her grandmother and her, even risking his life to remain with them when the hurricane had hit, instead of taking shelter in City Hall, where it was safer. He'd opened his own home to them, slept on the couch so they could have his bed, and not once had he complained. He'd gone out of his way once again by cleaning up Reba's place, and look what she'd given him in return. She took a deep breath and headed outside toward the boat.

If Gator heard her walk up, he didn't give any indication. Instead, he merely stared at the gently moving bayou, as though it held some great secret. Michelle picked her way cautiously across the grass, her eyes scanning the area for long, slithery creatures. She stopped at the water's edge.

"I made dinner," she said, her voice hopeful. A light breeze ruffled her hair, and she pushed aside a few strands. "Tuna fish and pork and beans," she added, "which I believe are favorites of yours."

Gator swung his head around slowly. The smile he offered was faint. "I don't believe I've ever had tuna fish and pork and beans in the same meal."

She nodded. "And if you're lucky, you won't ever have to do it again after tonight."

He chuckled and turned away.

She sighed heavily, clasping her hands in front of her. "Gator, I feel crummy about the things I said to you. I'm sorry."

"I had it coming," he said.

She figured that was as close to an apology that she would receive, but she was grateful nonetheless. "I know I haven't been easy to get along with at times," she went on. "I don't know what's gotten into me except ... well, I'm tired of eating canned food and washing up out of a sink. There's not much I wouldn't give for a hot bubble bath and clean hair, not to mention a bit of makeup. I never thought of myself as a vain person until this happened, but—" She paused. "None of that really matters. What's important here is that we work at getting along because I don't know how long we'll be stranded."

When Gator faced her again, he was grinning. He hadn't expected the apology, but he appreciated it just the same, and he had to admit he <u>had</u> pushed her. "So what exactly would you do for a bubble bath, Mic?"

She laughed. He was back to his old self again, thank goodness. She only hoped they could stay on friendly terms until help arrived. "I have maybe fifty dollars total in my purse," she said. "I think, at this point I'd be willing to part with some of that cash for a real, honest-to-goodness bubble bath. That's one reason I was looking forward to going to your mom's house."

Gator did not come in for dinner, which surprised Michelle, so she dined alone. She felt hot and gritty and tired, and there wasn't a muscle in her body that did not ache from all the hard work she had done the past couple of days. Perhaps if she rested a bit, but she was half afraid she would not wake up until morning, and she still had a few things she wanted to do before going to bed. Maybe if she closed her eyes for twenty minutes she would catch her second wind.

She curled up on the sofa and rested her eyes. Several times, she heard Gator come into the house, heard his footsteps on the stairs leading to the second floor, but she was too exhausted to get up and see if he needed her help with anything.

Gator finished what he was doing and walked over to the sofa where Michelle was sleeping. For a moment, all he could do was stare at the fetching picture she presented, her hair falling softly across her face, one hand tucked beneath her cheek. Her shorts gave him an unobstructed view of the loveliest legs he'd ever seen—trim ankles, shapely calves and thighs. Her blouse had worked its way up her rib cage again, exposing a wide band of silky-looking skin. Something stirred in his body, and he realized he'd become aroused simply by watching her sleep. He gently nudged her. "Wake up sleepyhead," he said.

Michelle opened her eyes and blinked several times. Gator was standing over her, a grin lighting his face. She sat up. "How long have I been asleep?"

"An hour. Maybe longer." His grin broadened. "I believe you mentioned wanting a bubble bath?"

She blinked again. "Uh-huh, but—"

"You're all set, kiddo. I couldn't find bubble bath, so I used dish detergent instead." He handed her a flashlight. "Just follow me."

Michelle stood and, still half asleep, followed him up the flight of stairs. He led her inside the old-fashioned bathroom, where a large decorative candle placed on the back of the toilet provided a cozy light. The tub was more than half filled with water. She touched it tentatively. “It’s hot,” she said in disbelief. “Where’d you get hot water?”

“I found an iron pot in one of the sheds,” he said, “and I heated the water over a camp fire. It ought to be just right so you’d better hop in.” He paused and pointed to a towel and a bottle of shampoo that he’d placed on the closed toilet lid. “I figured you’d need that. Call me after you wash your hair, and I’ll rinse it for you.” He reached for Reba’s bathrobe, which was hanging on the back of the bathroom door. “I figure you can put this on and lean over the sink.”

Having lived with no luxuries the past few days, Michelle was genuinely touched. “I don’t know what to say,” she confessed. “Thank you, Gator.”

“Just don’t let the water out when you’re finished,” he said. “I want to get in after you.” He turned for the door. “Call me when you want me to rinse your hair.” He disappeared, closing the bathroom door behind him.

Michelle stepped out of her clothes eagerly and left them in a neat pile on the bathroom floor. She sank slowly into the hot bathwater, filling the room with sighs of pleasure. At first she just lay there, allowing her aching muscles to soak in the heat. Gator Landry had outdone himself this time. She wondered how long it had taken him to heat the water in an old iron pot and carry it up the stairs. She could not have appreciated it more.

Once she had washed, she reached for a bucket beside the tub, wet her hair, and applied the shampoo. She took great joy working up a thick lather, scrubbing her hair and scalp thoroughly. Finally, she piled the long soapy strands on top of her head and stepped out of the tub. She dried herself briskly, mopping her face and neck where the shampoo trickled down. She pulled on Reba's robe.

Gator came into the bathroom as soon as she called to him, carrying another bucket of steaming water. He smiled at the sight of her in Reba's robe, a towel draped around her neck. Her skin glowed a healthy color. "Ready to rinse, ma'am?" he asked, testing the water in the bucket to make sure it wasn't too hot.

"Yes sir," she replied, leaning over the old pedestal sink. Gator poured the water over her head slowly and watched the shampoo bubbles wash down the drain. Although it took several buckets of water to rinse her long hair, Gator did not mind in the least. There was something very intimate about washing a woman's hair, he decided, and he liked it. The back of her neck was long and white and sprinkled with downy blond hairs that beckoned a man's lips. He tried to push the thought aside and concentrate on rinsing her golden mane.

Afterward, Michelle dried it with a towel and let it fall wet against her shoulders. Gator pondered if she knew how sexy she looked to him, or how sweet she smelled.

"This is the nicest thing anybody has ever done for me," she said, touching his arm gently.

Gator swallowed. Her touch was light, but he felt something inside him quicken at the feel of her hand on his bare arm, and her green eyes with their soft expression, told him how much she appreciated his efforts. "You didn't stay in very long," he said, his voice sounding strange to his own ears. "I figured you'd be in here awhile."

"I didn't want the water to get cold since you're planning on using it. If you like, I can try to find something for you to wear after your bath. My grandmother could not bear to get rid of my grandfather's clothes once he passed so she and I moved them to the closet in the spare bedroom. I'll see if I can find a bathrobe."

"Thanks," he said and handed her the flashlight. For a moment, they stood looking at one another. Michelle decided it was time she put some distance between them. The bathroom had suddenly grown too small, and it seemed to be lacking in oxygen. That probably explained why she felt breathless and light-headed. She hurried out and closed the door.

Gator shucked off his clothes and got into the

tub. The water was still warm. He scrubbed from head to toe. Once he washed his hair he realized there were no more buckets of warm water available so he rinsed in cold water beneath the bathtub faucet. Instead of feeling cold, it cooled his body temperature, and he did not feel so hot.

Michelle tapped on the door a few minutes later. "I'm leaving my grandfather's bathrobe outside the door."

"Thanks," Gator said.

She hesitated, listening to the sounds of Gator washing. Her mind was instantly filled with images of him sitting in the tub, his naked body slick and wet, the light from the candle illuminating those black eyes. She heard him climb from the tub and she hurried away.

Gator emerged from the bathroom a few minutes later, wearing the bathrobe and looking refreshed. Michelle thought he'd never looked sexier. The robe was short on him, the hem falling well above his knees, exposing a pair of hair-roughened calves and thighs that were lean but slightly muscular. She felt her stomach tighten at the sight of him. His wet hair fell about his head carelessly.

"Well, that certainly felt good," he announced, sinking on the couch beside her. The cushion dipped under the weight of his body. He leaned back and propped his feet on Reba's coffee table.

He smelled of soap and male flesh, Michelle noted, kicking her own feet up next to his, trying her darnedest to appear casual about the whole thing. But how could she hope to pull that off when her thoughts refused to cooperate? How was she supposed to forget that he was completely naked beneath that robe?

A large calico cat leaped into her lap and curled into a fat ball. For a moment Michelle and Gator merely sat there, both of them gazing at the candle she had place on the coffee table.

"When do you think someone will come for us?" she finally asked.

"In the morning probably."

"So we'll sleep here tonight?"

He nodded. "I don't know anyone dumb enough to venture out on the bayou at night."

"I hope Reba isn't worried."

"She knows I'll take care of you, Mic," he said gently.

Michelle raised her green eyes to his black ones. She knew he spoke the truth. Reba might be concerned when she didn't return, but she would feel comfortable knowing Gator was with her. And the odd thing about it was Michelle felt equally comfortable. Gator, in his own way, inspired confidence. He might make her mad as at times, but she knew she was safe in his care. She smiled at the thought.

Gator didn't miss it. "What're you thinking, Mic?" he asked softly.

"I was just wondering how on earth you came up with a nickname like Gator." Actually, she was trying to come up with something to take her mind off his nearness. It wasn't an easy task.

He chuckled. "How do you know that's not my real name?"

"Reba told me your real name was Matthieu."

He arched one dark brow. "So you were asking Reba about me?"

She blushed. "No. Reba mentioned it the day of the storm when you arrived in your boat." She shot him a sideways glance. "So how'd you get the name?"

He shrugged. "I once raised a baby alligator from birth. The kids called me Alligator Man for a while, and then just shortened it to Gator. I never cared much for my real name anyway."

"I like it."

He turned to her. "You do? Well, that's a first. You finally discovered something about me you like."

His words surprised her. "I've always liked you, Gator," she said. "I just don't understand you, that's all. You're so ... different from the other men I know."

He faced her, propping his elbow on the back of the couch. Michelle tensed when his robe fell open slightly, exposing part of his chest. He didn't seem to notice.

Gator studied her in the flickering candlelight. It accentuated the lovely contours of her face, bringing out her high cheekbones and emphasizing her wide green eyes. She had never looked lovelier. "Is that so bad, to be different from other people?"

Michelle took a long time answering, not only because it was difficult concentrating with him so close, but because she felt her answer was important. Maybe it would explain to both of them why their relationship was so tense. "Not bad, I guess. I just feel ... unsure about myself when I'm with you. I never know what to expect." And she never knew what to expect from herself, she wanted to add.

"So you don't like surprises, huh?" He smiled gently.

"I like knowing where I stand with a person."

He pondered her remark. "I've always thought highly of you," he said. He reached for a lock of damp hair and rubbed it between his fingers. She didn't seem to mind. "Even though we were never intimate, I never forgot how you smelled, how your mouth tasted when I kissed you. I've never experienced that sort of thing with another woman."

"It didn't stop you from trying, though, right?" she asked, offering him a wry smile.

"I never had any reason not to." He wound the lock of hair around his index finger. "You were special, Mic," he said simply and honestly.

"Too bad I had no way of knowing that."

"You had just turned sixteen. What was I supposed to do?"

"Sixteen years have passed since that summer, Gator. That's a long time."

He released her hair and let his hand fall to her shoulder. "Mic, if I had thought for one minute you were interested in hearing from me—" He didn't finish the sentence.

"I thought you'd at least write."

"I wanted to, believe me."

"But you didn't."

"I was scared."

"You? Scared?" She looked doubtful. "I can't believe Gator Landry would be scared of anything."

His eyes held hers tight. "I'm scared to death right now, Mic." At her look of surprise, he went on. "I'm scared about all these feelings that come to the surface when I look at you. I'm scared because of the things I want to say to you, of the things I want to do to you."

His words sucked the breath right out of her. "What ... things?"

"Things like—" He hesitated. "Like maybe I fell in love with you that summer," he finally said. "I know I was young at the time, but I think I loved you just the same. Sometimes you just know these things. You know when a person has touched you. And, despite the passing of time, those feelings never went away." He raised a finger to her neck and stroked the white skin there, finding it incredibly soft. "I must've made love to you a million times in my dreams," he confessed.

Michelle shivered at the sound of his voice; her skin prickled as his fingers trickled up her neck and traced her ear. She attempted to smile, but she could feel her bottom lip tremble with the effort. "And did you ... enjoy it?"

"More than you'll ever know."

For a moment, all they could do was stare at each other. Michelle knew he was going to kiss her, and she couldn't have moved if she'd wanted to. His gaze held her rooted to the spot. He lowered his face to hers slowly and hesitated one heart-stopping moment before touching his lips to hers.

She had been waiting for him to kiss her, Michelle realized, and when his tongue prodded her lips open, she was only too happy to oblige. She met the thrust of his tongue boldly, and the kiss deepened and became more erotic than anything she had ever experienced. He sampled the textures of her mouth, sliding his tongue across her teeth and dipping into the dark nooks and crannies as though searching for a hidden treasure. He took her bottom lip between his teeth and tugged it gently, then raised his calloused palms to her face and turned her head just so, giving him free access to her mouth. Michelle had never been so thoroughly kissed in her life.

Gator paused briefly so they could gulp air into their lungs, then, he captured her lips once more, at the same time trying to hold himself in check so that he didn't rush the moment. He wanted it to last forever, but he was already so aroused that he couldn't think straight. He raised his head and looked at her. When he spoke, his voice was raw with emotion. "If you are going to stop me, do it now, Mic."

Michelle was almost frightened by the intensity of his gaze. "Gator, I can't think—"

"The time for thinking is over, Mic," he said gruffly. "You either want me or you don't." He gazed at her for a moment, feeling as vulnerable as he ever had in his life. He was almost crazy from wanting her, but he wasn't about to make the first move. This was what 16 years of dreaming about her had done to him. It was scary to want a woman that much.

Michelle slipped her arms around his neck and pulled him close, so close his lips brushed hers as lightly as a butterfly's wing. Heat radiated from his body. "I do want you, Gator," she whispered against his mouth. "I've always wanted you."

Chapter Six

Gator gazed at her for several seconds as the full measure of her words sank in. Her eyes were soft with invitation, her slight smile beguiling and sexy as all get-out. He leaned his head forward, touching her nose playfully with his own, the look in his eyes saying more than he possibly could at the moment. He stood, reached for her hand and tugged gently. Michelle came to her feet. Gator paused briefly, reached for the large ornamental candle he'd carried from the bathroom and led the way to the stairs.

Once they reached the top, Michelle pointed toward the guest room. Gator followed her direction and set the candle on the night table beside the bed. The room was bathed in a golden light that made it appear warm and cozy. Michelle noticed that Reba's old furniture didn't look as harsh in the soft light; but she could not have cared less. The only thing she cared about was the man standing before her.

Gator stared at Michelle as though she were an apparition, which wasn't far from the truth as far as he was concerned. If someone had told him a week ago that he'd be sharing her bed, he would have laughed. He still couldn't believe it. Surely he had done something good in his life to deserve this.

"Take off the robe, Mic," he said gently. "I've waited sixteen years to see you, and I can't stand it any longer." When she hesitated, he added, "Please."

Michelle reached for the tie on her grandmother's robe and tugged the knot free. She pulled the garment open, slid it from her shoulders, and let it fall to the floor.

Gator heard his own quick intake of breath as he greedily devoured the woman before him with his eyes—the gentle sloping shoulders, the high, softly rounded breasts, and dark coral nipples. Her waist dipped at her navel, then flared into perfectly proportioned hips. The dark blond tuft at the base of her thighs sent a tremor through his body and a rumble of pleasure low in his chest. He raised his eyes to her face. She looked so vulnerable, so unsure, as though she feared she wouldn't measure up. He didn't know what to make of it, but he knew the last thing he needed to do was rush her, even though his body cried out for her.

"It was worth waiting sixteen years, Mic," he

said. He opened his arms, and she went willingly.

His mouth was warm and soft, giving way to a kiss that was gentle and caring and blessedly unhurried. Michelle leaned into the embrace, drawing strength from his big body and confidence with each gentle, slow-handed caress. She could feel Gator holding back, taking his time with her, and she appreciated it.

Soon, the kisses turned hot and frantic, Gator's tongue more insistent. He pressed his mouth against the hollow of her throat, where her pulse beat wildly. He moved to an earlobe, nipped it gently, and then dipped his tongue inside. Michelle shivered.

Gator had cautioned himself not to hurry. He wanted to savor each moment and give Michelle time to relax with him, but he could not look at her without touching her. He raised his hands slowly and covered each breast with an open palm. Her skin looked like fine porcelain against his dark hands. Finally, he lowered his head.

Michelle slipped her fingers through his unruly black hair, holding his face close as his lips and tongue toyed with each nipple. For a moment, she merely held him there, stroking his hair as a feeling of tenderness washed over her. Then slowly, the feeling was replaced with something more intense and erotic, warming her lower belly and spiraling downward, congregating at the juncture of her thighs. She trembled with pleasure and anticipation.

Gator shrugged out of his own robe, and Michelle gazed at him, thinking if a man's body could be described as beautiful, Gator would win the prize hands-down. There wasn't an ounce of fat on the man, only brown flesh and tight muscle. She touched his chest lightly, running her hands through the springy curls that grasped her fingers like silken rings.

"Touch me, Mic," he said simply.

Michelle complied, gently closing her palm around him.

Gator closed his eyes. How many times had he felt her do just that in his dreams? His blood roared in his ears as she began a gentle lover's caress that in a matter of seconds had him hard and ready for her. "Not yet, Mic," he said, stilling her small hand with his. Taking her into his arms once more, Gator eased Michelle onto the bed, following as she went, the mattress dipping under their weight. Once again, he moved his mouth to her breasts, then inched his way to her navel, swirling his tongue around her belly button. Then he kissed his way to her concave stomach. His hands never quieted, stroking and tantalizing her flesh. Finally, he probed the curls between her thighs and dipped his fingers inside. He grinned when he found what he wanted. She was wet.

“Oh, baby,” he moaned. His black eyes glittered in the candlelight.

Michelle sighed with ultimate pleasure as Gator’s fingers made contact with the very root of her desire. She arched against his hand, letting her thighs fall to the side as he worked his magic. And even as her inhibitions tried to keep her from losing control, Gator whispered words of encouragement—some of them sweet and tender, others demanding and erotic enough to bring a rosy blush to her cheeks and send her over the edge.

Heat surged through her, and a feeling of such pleasure gripped her that Michelle cried out. She trembled as Gator moved over her. He waited for her to guide him to her center, then he gently pressed forward until she had buried himself inside.

For a moment, Gator merely lay there, his body propped on his elbows. He gazed down at Michelle and thought she had never looked lovelier, her green eyes soft, her smile tender. He kissed her lightly on the lips and very slowly began to move inside her. She was hot and tight, gripping him, making him crazy with desire. He kissed her again, deeply, and her tongue met his eagerly, just as her hips met his steady thrusts. They moved in unison, as though in time to the same dance tune, hard lines complementing soft curves. He heard her breath quicken. As before, she cried out his name and arched against him. He gave one finale thrust, hovered on the brink, then shuddered.

When Gator finally raised his head from her shoulder, he was smiling. Actually, he was grinning from ear to ear, as though over some private joke.

"What's so funny?" Michelle asked.

Gator didn't answer right away. Instead, he rolled aside and gathered her into his arms. He sighed, and the sound was one of pure male satisfaction. "I was just thinking what a shame it was that we let all those years pass us by before we finally got together. And to think, it took a damn hurricane to do it." He sighed again, this time wistfully. "All that good lovin' we missed out on. Kind of makes you sad, doesn't it?" He stroked the back of her neck as he talked.

Michelle frowned. How could Gator be so casual about what had just happened between them, when for her, the earth had moved. He'd simply referred to it as a bit of "good lovin'." Her gaze fluttered up his chest to his face.

"What's wrong, Mic?"

She could not keep the annoyance out of her voice. "I think lovemaking is highly overrated in a relationship, Gator," she said. "It's important, but it's not everything." There now. She could be just as casual about it as the next person.

Gator knew a moment of intense disappointment. But what could he expect? Just because their lovemaking was the greatest thing that had ever happened to him didn't mean it had been the same for her. "Well, you certainly seemed to be taking it seriously a moment ago," he muttered.

Michelle's face flamed. Wasn't it just like Gator Landry to poke fun at her? Why had she thought their lovemaking would alter him, anyway? She pulled away, but he refused to let her go. Instead, he laughed and pulled her tighter against him.

"I'm just teasing you, honey," he said. "I like a passionate woman. In fact, I prefer it." That wasn't entirely true, he reminded himself. He wanted her to tell him she wasn't normally so passionate, that <u>he</u> had been the reason for that passion; he needed her to suggest that he had done and made her feel extraordinary things, things like he was feeling.

"You're laughing at me, Gator. You're always laughing at me."

He was clearly surprised by her outburst. "I'm not laughing at you, honey. I was just teasing. There's nothing wrong with having a little fun in bed, is there?"

"You're always laughing at me," she repeated, "wearing that grin ... that cocky smile ... you're doing it right now, Gator Landry," she said, pointing an accusing finger at him.

"Gee, Mic, I didn't realize—" He paused and his look sobered. "I don't do it on purpose. I'll admit I sometimes lose my train of thought when I'm with you, and my mind sort of goes off in another direction. Sometimes my thoughts get a little X-rated. Maybe that's what makes me smile." He shrugged. "I just can't think straight when you're around. You make me edgy."

"*I* make *you* edgy?" she echoed in disbelief.

He nodded. "Hell yeah, you make me edgy. Here I am trying to concentrate on getting this town put back together, and you're flittin' around in those tight shorts of yours and that blouse that shows your cute little belly button every time you raise your arms. How'm I suppose to get any work done, for Pete's sake?"

For a moment, she merely stared at him. It was nice to believe she tempted him just a little. And it was flattering to know she could make Gator Landry want her after all these years. It gave her a feeling of confidence that she hadn't known in a long time. She raised her hand to Gator's magnificent chest. "So I'm a distraction to you, huh?" she teased.

"You might say that. And it's annoying as hell sometimes. It's sort of like having an itch you can't reach." He shot her a devilish grin and captured her hand with his. He squeezed it once and raised it to his face then kissed her palm. She thought lovemaking was overrated, did she? Well, he would show her just how important healthy sex was between a man and a woman. He would make love to her till her toes curled, until her hair stood on end. And when he was finished with her, she would know she'd been made love to by Gator Landry.

Their lovemaking was slow and leisurely, and when Gator pulled Michelle on top of him, he filled her completely, loving the way she fit around him so intimately. He moved against her slowly, torturing her—every time she came close to climax, he went completely still. Finally, she cried out, pleading with him not to stop. He gave her what she wanted, thrusting into her with a vengeance that surprised even him. She would not forget him soon, he promised her silently. By the time his groan of pleasure drifted upward, she was totally spent from several releases.

Afterward, he kissed her deeply, unable to tear his lips away from hers. He thought it odd because he'd never been much for kissing, other than the few obligatory kisses before and after sex. But he wanted to kiss Michelle, he realized. In fact, he enjoyed it immensely.

They fell into an exhausted sleep in each other's arms.

Chapter Seven

When Gator opened his eyes the following morning, he found Michelle watching him from her pillow. He smiled and stretched, then reached for her and pulled her into his arms. "G'morning, Beautiful. How'd you sleep?"

"We have to talk."

Gator blinked at the seriousness of her voice. "Is something wrong?"

"Something is very wrong," she said. "We didn't practice safe sex last night."

He blinked again. "You mean you might be pregnant?"

She rolled her eyes and rose up. "Of course not, but we didn't do anything to prevent... well ... you know."

He shook his head, looking suddenly amused. "No, I don't know. You tell me."

"We could have passed something on; a disease. Neither of us was protected."

The smile faded as he sat up. "Oh, I get it. You're afraid I gave you something, right?" He was surprised how much the idea stung. He swung his legs off the bed and stood, planting a hand on one outthrust hip as though totally unaware of his nakedness. Michelle thought he had never looked more magnificent, with the early-morning light bathing his skin. "I'll bet you didn't stop and ask your good doctor if he was free from cooties before you let him make love with you."

"You're wrong about that."

He ignored her comment. Damn, but she knew how to get the morning off to a crappy start. He felt as if she'd just poured ice water over his head. "But I'm not a hotshot doctor, so I'm not good enough for you, right? I'm okay for cleaning up your grandmother's property and running you all over town in my truck, but I'm not safe to go to bed with. Is that the way it is, Mic?" For the first time Gator realized he was shouting, and he lowered his voice. "You don't have anything to worry about, princess. I'm clean." He grabbed his robe and slammed out of the room, literally shaking the house.

Michelle followed, her chest filling with anger. She threw open the bedroom door and ran to the top of the stairs. "Gator Landry, don't you just walk out on me and slam the door in my face. Who do you think you are?"

Gator paused near the middle of the stairs. He

turned around slowly and made his way back up, his head hitched high, his black eyes cool. "Who do you think you are?"

"I'm a grown woman," she said, "who usually gives more thought to simply falling into bed with a man. But last night—" She paused. "I don't know what got into me. I wasn't thinking." He didn't understand. She could see that he was offended. "I've traveled all over the state with other nurses speaking to young men and women about using caution where sex is concerned. I keep a supply of condoms in my purse at all times."

He looked surprised. "You keep rubbers in your purse?"

"I certainly do. It's a habit I suggest other women pick up as well."

He cocked his head to the side and regarded her. "How long does it take you to go through a box of, say, a dozen?" he asked. He wasn't sure he felt comfortable with the thought that she was always prepared for sex.

"That's not important."

He arched one brow. "It is to me."

"The point is I'm always protected. I can't afford to take risks, and neither can you."

Some of his anger abated when he realized she wasn't attacking him personally. Not that he blamed her, of course. His reputation wasn't the best. And in this day and age, she had every right to be cautious. He shouldn't have blown his stack so quickly and taken offense. Gator climbed the stairs slowly and paused one step below her. She had thrown on her robe carelessly, without tying it. He let his eyes take in the vertical slit of skin that peeked through.

"I always protect myself, Mic," he finally said. "I just didn't feel I had to with you." His eyes locked with hers. "You're safe with me, honey, I swear, but if you want me to get tested for STDs, I'll do it immediately. Today."

For some reason, she believed him. Gator Landry might have his faults, but she could not imagine him taking chances with her health or life. "I'm sorry I had to bring it up."

He fingered the tie on her robe. "You were right to," he said. "I shouldn't have gotten so riled up over it." He paused and smiled. "You think maybe I could borrow from your stash?" he asked, his eyes full of mischief. "I seem to be short at the moment. Unless, of course, you've used them all."

She slapped him playfully. "It's a brand-new box, silly. I haven't even used the first one."

"Mind if I ask how long you've had that box?"

She regarded him. "Why?"

"'Cause I'm a selfish bastard with double standards, that's why."

She smiled softly. There was something to be said for honesty. "I've had it for almost six months now."

He was pleased with her answer, and it showed. "I didn't have any right to ask."

"I know."

"Why'd you tell me?"

She shrugged. "Because I have nothing to hide. But I would have expected you to accept an alternative answer as well."

He nodded. "I'd like to think I would have accepted it, Mic, but I can't swear to it. I'm jealous and selfish, and I know it. I prefer to think you've been sitting around all these years waiting for me."

"I'd like to think the same of you, Gator, but I know that's not likely."

He reached for her, slipping his big hands inside her robe, where she was still warm from sleep. Her long hair was tousled about her head. "I want to make love to you again, Michelle Thurston," he said simply.

She smiled softly. "And I want you to make love to me, Matthieu Landry."

He gazed at her for a moment, liking the way she said his name. It sounded low and sexy on Michelle's lips. They could not get up the stairs quickly enough.

#

Reba Kenner and Fiona Landry sat on the cozy, fern-filled front porch and sipped their coffee while

Mae West warmed herself in a pool of early morning sun. Reba drained her coffee cup and set it on the little wicker table nearby.

"You reckon we should send someone after them?"

Fiona shrugged. "No need to rush."

"What if they kill each other? They fight like cats and dogs sometimes."

Fiona laughed. "Michelle's a nurse, isn't she? If either of them gets hurt, she should be able to take care of it."

"What do you think they're doing?"

"Who knows? A man and woman all alone out there in the bayou ..." She paused, and her face took on a dreamy-eyed expression. "So romantic."

Reba crossed her arms. "It won't be romantic if they find out we paid someone five dollars to add a little water to that gas tank."

Fiona waved the statement aside. "They won't find out. Besides, we did them a favor. Those two have been crazy about each other for years, but they're too blasted stubborn to do anything about it. We just gave them a gentle nudge. They'll thank us in the end. And one day we'll all look back on it and laugh."

"Does that mean one day you'll tell 'em what we did?"

"No. This secret is going with me to the grave. "

"So what time should we send someone after

them?"

"Let's not rush things."

#

Gator removed the sizzling meat from the frying pan and placed it on the plate Michelle held in her hand. "Breakfast is served, ma'am," he announced with a flourish. He then moved the frying pain from his camp fire and put on a pan of water to boil so they could have instant coffee.

Michelle gazed at the fried Spam dully. Oh, what she'd give for a stack of buttermilk pancakes dripping with butter and syrup, and a tall glass of cold milk, she thought. "I'll carry this inside," she said, trying to muster a little enthusiasm over their meager breakfast. "I found half a loaf of bread in the pantry that's still good."

Gator followed her into the house and to the kitchen, where Michelle had laid out plates and silverware on the small table. He waited for her to sit down, then took the chair across from her. She forked the meat onto their plates and handed him the package of bread. He took it, but his gaze was trained on her. She'd combed her hair, and it lay against her shoulders like a silken curtain. He still remembered how it had felt between his fingers as he'd rinsed the shampoo from it the night before, how it had felt against his shoulder. After the lovemaking they'd shared, it was impossible for him to look at her without wanting her.

Michelle glanced up from her plate and caught him staring. She smiled. "What are you thinking?"

He shrugged. "I'm thinking how much I'd like to take you to a nice steak restaurant."

"Steak?" She said the word reverently. "Do you think we'll ever eat fresh meat and vegetables again?"

He grinned. "I'm counting on it."

She sighed wistfully. "Do you think life will ever return to normal after this?"

He met her gaze. "Not for me."

She knew he spoke the truth. They could repair the power lines and get the town back on its feet after the storm, but life would never be the same. In the past few days, especially in the last twelve hours, her life had changed dramatically. No, things would never be the same after Gator Landry.

Michelle took a bite of her sandwich and chewed, but she was uncomfortably aware that Gator was watching her. "What are you going to do when this is over?" she asked. "When things are as normal as they're going to get."

Gator pondered her question. "Well, first I'm going to clean up this one area in town where we have a lot of trouble. I'd already started doing it, but the storm sort of put matters on hold. There's a couple of kids who are real troublemakers and—" He stopped. "'Course there's not much for a kid to do in this town. You know? We only have one theater, and it plays the same movie for weeks at a time. This place is really hard up for entertainment. It's no surprise the kids get into trouble."

"Don't you have a YMCA?"

"Yeah, but there's not much to it. We don't have the funds."

"You should ask for volunteers. And more money so you can start a youth program," she added. "If the crime rate here among kids has picked up, then you have every right to go to City Hall and ask for help with the problem. The program I'm involved with is strictly on a volunteer basis. We travel throughout the state and speak on issues concerning young people. Not just diseases, mind you. We talk about alcohol and drugs, bullying, and the importance of a good education. And it's all done on a voluntary basis. I could check on the possibility of having your parish included in our tour."

"That's all fine and dandy, Mic, but I don't want the responsibility." At her look of surprise, he went on. "Not that I don't want the best for this town," he said, "but I don't want to be the one to do it. I have other plans for my life."

She nodded. "I know. Have you got someone in mind to take over?"

"There are a couple of good deputies who might be interested. I didn't really have a chance to discuss it with them before the storm hit and everything went to hell around here. Before that, I was mainly concerned about finding out who'd robbed my mother. You see, I had planned to use my badge to get back at him. Throw him in jail for ninety days with only bread and water, that sort of thing."

"I don't think you can legally do that."

"Yeah, I know. And it's not a reason to take a job you don't want in the first place. I was more interested in revenge at the time, I suppose. But my mother is all I have left in this world."

"How come you never married and had children?" She knew she was being nosy, but couldn't help it. She wanted to know more about the man, had to know more. She should have known that sleeping with him would bring out this curious, involved and caring side of her.

"I never had anything to offer a woman. And when I worked the sugar cane fields ... well, there wasn't room in my life for anything else."

"Tell me about it."

He shrugged. "I was just traveling through when I came upon this place, all run-down. The old man who owned it laughed in my face when I asked for a job. He said he hadn't had a decent crop in years. We were both in bad shape. He couldn't keep good help, and I couldn't find a job 'cause of my bad record with juvenile justice. So I offered to help him out in exchange for room and board. It took a long time to get the place on its feet again. I would have left long before, had I not gotten attached to the old guy. He became a father figure to me. The place started making money, lots of it. He made me a full partner."

"Do you ever hear from him?"

"He passed away while I was still there. Left everything to me, including his house. I didn't feel like staying after he died so I sold everything and hit the road."

"Are you rich?"

Gator grinned. "I'm set up nicely."

"So when do you plan to marry and start a family?" she asked.

"I haven't thought much about it," he said. "You?"

"I was almost engaged, but it didn't work out."

"To Jeffrey?"

"How did you guess?"

"What happened?"

She shrugged. "He had the ring and everything, but I told him I needed more time, even though we had been dating exclusively for almost a year."

"Is that why he cheated?"

"That was the excuse he used, but who knows, he could have been seeing other women all along. Behind my back," she added.

Gator frowned. "And you're still friends with this

Yahoo?"

"I forgave him."

"So what happens after the baby comes and he wants out of his so-called unhappy marriage?"

"That's none of my business." Michelle decided a change of subject was in order. "You've heard my story. What's yours?"

"I've never been engaged. I've never even dated steadily." He shrugged. "To be honest, I don't like the idea of changing and rearranging my life to meet someone else's needs. See, I told you I was selfish. I've always done exactly what I wanted. A wife and family would complicate matters."

"You're right," she said. "That's what happens when you allow another person into your world." Michelle picked up her saucer and carried it to the sink.

Gator's chair scraped the floor as he shoved away from the table. Picking up his own cup and saucer, he crossed the room, closing the distance between them. He stood behind Michelle for a moment, his body only inches from hers. She felt him there, he knew. He could tell by the way she held herself so still. He took another step and reached around her to set the dishes in the sink. She jumped when the plate made contact with the porcelain.

Michelle could feel the heat of his body, feel the hairs on the back of her neck rise. She closed her eyes when he pressed himself against her. "What are you doing?" she asked breathlessly. She could hear the laughter in his voice when he spoke, could feel his need pressing into her hips.

"I'm trying to seduce you. How am I doing?"

She could not help but smile. "I think you're turning yourself on at my expense."

"Turn around, Mic," he said softly. When she didn't budge, he rolled his eyes heavenward. "Please," he added.

Michelle faced him, and then wished she hadn't. He was so close, so uncomfortably close, she could see the stubble on his unshaven face. She tried to take a step back, but her hips met the cabinet. Gator placed his hands on the countertop on each side of her, leaning forward slightly, his breath fanning her cheek.

"You make me crazy, Michelle Thurston, you know that? Even when we were little more than kids." He pressed his body against hers as he spoke, and her pelvis cradled his. "Every time you're near I get this urge to throw you over my shoulder and whisk you off to my cave. Yes, I said cave," he added with a chuckle. "I guess you bring out the beast in me, huh?" When she didn't speak, he raised a finger to her lips and brushed them gently. "Is that so bad, Mic? To want to have a little control over the woman you're crazy about?"

"A relationship should be fifty-fifty," she said with conviction.

He grinned. "Is that how they talk at cocktail parties and luncheons these days? All that sounds good, but there are times when a man wants to be in charge. Call it ego, I don't care, but sometimes a man likes to feel as though he is the protector. That it's up to him to take care of his woman."

"You're a man of contradictions, Gator. On one hand, you don't want a woman setting foot in your perfect life and messing things up. But if a woman happens to catch your fancy, you want to run the show, have things you're way. What about *her* needs? Why does *anyone* have to be in charge? Why can't two people who love each other be on equal footing?"

The smile he gave her was slow and lazy. "You think you've got it all figured out, don't you?"

She leveled her gaze at him. "I know what I want in *my* life, but I can't speak for you."

Chapter Eight

Gator saw the challenge in her green eyes and hitched his chin higher. "I reckon at my age I know how to keep a woman happy, Mic."

"In the bedroom, maybe," she replied evenly, "but people can't stay in bed all day. What have you got to offer a woman outside the sheets, Gator? There are many facets of a woman, you know. She likes to be charmed and courted."

"I can charm the fur off a possum at nine hundred yards, babe."

Although Michelle liked the endearment, she realized Gator wasn't taking her seriously. "And when you're finished in the bedroom, there is another side to a relationship you haven't considered; the day-to-day responsibilities, the grocery store, the dry cleaner, housework, yard work—"

"You sure know how to cool a man's ardor," he said.

"Sex is important, but it should be like a fine dessert in a relationship. Everything else has to be good between two people for the sex to be good."

"You make it sound like a job, Mic. That takes all the fun out of it. Why can't two people just enjoy what they have while it lasts?"

"Because the better you work at it, the more enjoyable it is, and the longer it lasts. Perhaps forever."

"Forever?" He looked skeptical. "That's a long time. I can't think past next week. I don't want my life so neatly planned, Mic." He shoved his hands in his pockets and walked to one of the windows that had survived the storm and wasn't covered with plastic sheeting. A fine mist hovered over the bayou. "I suppose the good doctor couldn't meet all your needs after all, huh?"

Michelle didn't answer right away. "He came closer than some."

He faced her. "And how was dessert?"

Michelle's face turned red. "That's personal."

"This whole conversation is personal, Mic. But you brought it up, and you don't seem to mind exposing my faults. I guess I'm just trying to understand you better. Figure out exactly what you want in a man." He had no idea why he was going to so much trouble. He obviously couldn't come close to meeting her standards, and he wasn't sure he wanted to. The mere thought of tying himself down to one woman for the rest of his life was unnerving. And what about all those domestic chores she'd mentioned? Why buy groceries when you could eat out? And a man didn't have to worry about yard work when he lived on a houseboat.

Michelle was still pondering his question. She sighed. "Dessert with Jeffrey was like apple pie without ice cream or whipped cream on top."

"Meaning something was missing," Gator said. A million questions sprang to mind, but he didn't voice them. He had no right. Instead, he thrust one hip to the side and cocked his head. "So what is it like with me, Mic? Dessert, that is."

"You know it was good."

Male ego prodded him on. "But what would you compare it to?"

Michelle wished she'd never said anything about dessert. She had simply tried to make a point. But she knew Gator wouldn't let up until she told him. "Well, with you it's more like ..." She paused and smiled. "A hot fudge sundae with all the trimmings."

"Is that good?"

"Of course it's good. You have the hot fudge on one hand, nice and warm and gooey. Then there's the shivery-cold ice cream, the crunchiness of nuts, and the ultimate sweetness of whipped cream. It delights all the senses. What more could you ask for in a dessert?"

He chuckled and slowly closed the distance between them. He stood before her, gazing down at her and thinking how lovely she looked in the morning, her face the color of fresh cream. "I've never gotten aroused simply by listening to the ingredients of a hot fudge sundae," he mused aloud. He reached for a strand of hair and rubbed it between his fingers. "What d'you say we grab a can of whipped cream and go upstairs?"

Michelle laughed, but came willingly into his arms. She had grown tired of debating relationships when it was obvious that neither of them had been particularly successful in the happily-ever-after part. He nuzzled her ear, and she shivered and slipped her arms around his waist. He pulled away, his smile gone. His expression was almost tender.

"Mic, I can't do all those things. You know, the grocery store and dry cleaners. Parent-teacher conferences."

She cocked her head to one side. "Who said anything about parent-teacher conferences?"

"It all leads to that, Mic. Once a couple marries, they can't wait to have a baby, and that leads to a whole new set of responsibilities. Doctor visits, braces, play dates, first day of school. Sooner or later someone is going to have to go to a parent-teacher conference. That doesn't mean I'm not wild about you. Hell, I think I've been in love with you for sixteen years, but I'm especially not good at—"

She pressed her fingers against his lips. "I haven't asked anything of you."

He looked surprised. "Oh, well, that's a relief," he said when she removed her finger. He shook his head. "Lord, I want to make love to you so bad I hurt. I can't look at you without wanting to touch you. And I can't touch you without wanting to taste you. You're like an addiction, Mic." He smiled ruefully. "I have no right to make love to you, though. I have nothing to offer, nothing that really matters to a woman like you."

He paused and gazed down at her. Then, because he couldn't help himself, he lowered his lips to hers. He kissed her deeply, his tongue delving into her mouth hungrily. He wanted her. He wanted to sink into her softness and bury his face between her breasts. And it didn't matter that he'd only recently left her bed. When he raised his head, his eyes seemed to glow with passion.

Michelle snaked her arms around his neck. "I suppose," she said softly knowing that she wanted him to make love to her again just as badly. She couldn't get enough of the man.

It wasn't purely sexual between them, she knew, but Gator Landry would never admit it. He opened up to her when they were in bed, something he had difficulty doing otherwise. In her arms, he revealed himself for what he truly was—kind and loving and very giving. But she knew he was hell-bent on preserving his independent, tough-as-nails image. Gator had a gentle side that tugged at her heartstrings and wouldn't let go. And although he might balk at the idea of spending too much time with one woman, she knew he was hers in bed. For one heart-stopping moment, as he shuddered against her, he was totally and completely hers. And she didn't need false promises from him.

Gator took her hand and led her upstairs. When Michelle was completely naked, she began taking his clothes off of him. A moment later they were both on the bed, instantly swept up in a tide of passion that left them clinging to each other afterward.

#

Gator held her for a long time, listening to the sound of his own heartbeat, interrupted here and there by birdcalls from outside the window. When he spoke, his voice was tender. "I want you to know this has been the best two days of my life," he confessed. He squeezed her. "Thank you, Mic." He pondered his own words. He'd never thanked a woman for sharing a bed, but she'd given him more than a good time. He sensed she'd given herself as well. Compared to that, a simple thank you didn't seem enough.

Michelle was genuinely touched by his words,

but she didn't answer right away. She didn't trust her voice at the moment. Her heart ached, knowing that in a matter of time she would have to leave. She felt Gator truly loved her, had loved her for years, just as she had loved him. Yes, loved him, she told herself. She was in love with Gator Landry; it was as simple as that.

She rose up on one elbow and smiled into the handsome face. "I should be thanking you." It wasn't often a man made a woman feel the way he had made her feel. Gator had touched her in ways that other men hadn't come close, both physically and emotionally. She would always have a special place in her heart just for him, a place that she would protect. After all, he'd been the man who had awakened her body, brought sweet yearnings to the surface. The experience had been as delicious as it was scary, and it was the real reason she hadn't returned the following summer as she'd promised, the reason she'd avoided him completely on subsequent visits to her grandmother's.

She had known, even at the age of sixteen, that despite their wild attraction to each other, nothing could become of their relationship. Even at eighteen, Gator's need for independence had been firmly embedded in his personality. He might chase her relentlessly, but he would always remain just beyond her grasp.

A grinding noise broke through the silence in the

room, jarring Michelle from her thoughts. Gator rose from the bed and walked to the window, unabashed in his nakedness. “A boat,” he said. “Somebody finally decided to come for us.”

Michelle was thankful, almost.

#

“Well, they don’t look any different,” Reba said to Fiona as Gator and Michelle climbed out of his pickup truck and headed for the house.

Fiona Landry blushed. “Shhh, they’ll hear you!”

Reba planted her spindly hands on her hips and regarded the two with an amused look. “It’s a crying shame when you got to send the rescue squad out to pick up folks just ‘cause they ain’t got enough sense to come home when they’re s’posed to.”

“I hope you didn’t worry, Mom,” Gator said. “We would have been back yesterday had there not been a problem with the gas tank on the boat.”

Fiona waved the remark aside. “Oh, I wasn’t worried. There’s not a soul alive who knows the bayou better than you. Now, the two of you come up here on the porch and have something cold to drink while we still have ice. I bought a bag this morning. It should last until tomorrow.” Fiona smiled at Michelle. “You look cute as a button in that ponytail,” she said. “I hope my son has been behaving himself.”

Michelle blushed. If only the woman knew. A

brief picture of Gator and herself tangled in the bed sheets flashed through her mind. “Yes, he was a perfect gentleman.” She didn’t see the look of disappointment on the ladies’ faces, nor the amusement lurking in Gator’s eyes.

“Have some of my sugar cookies,” Fiona said, holding out a plate once Michelle was seated in one of the rocking chairs. “I made them the night before the storm, just in case we lost power and I couldn’t bake for a spell.” Fiona looked at Gator. “Sit here next to Michelle, Son, and tell Reba and me all about your adventures the last couple of days.”

“There’s not much to tell,” Gator said. He looked at Reba. “We were able to get a lot accomplished in your house and yard.”

“Oh, thank you for all you’ve done,” Reba said. “How are my cats?”

“They’re perfectly fine,” Michelle replied. “I left them plenty of food and water, plus I found a box that would hold extra kitty litter. They should be good for several days.”

“Reba is going to stay with me for a while,” Fiona said. “No way am I letting her go home to a damp house that has no electricity. We’ll see that her cats are cared for.” She looked from Gator to Mic and back at Gator. “It all sounds very dull, all that cleaning.”

“Yes, indeed,” Reba agreed. “Very dull.”

“I killed a snake,” Gator said. “I reckon that’s the

most exciting thing that happened." He turned to Michelle for confirmation. "Wouldn't you say?"

She almost choked on her cookie. "Uh, yes." She offered a faint smile. "A cottonmouth," she added to cover her embarrassment.

Fiona patted Michelle's hand. "I'll bet you were scared to death, honey," she said. "But it's over now and thank goodness nobody got bit. In the meantime, I paid a kid five dollars to dig a hole in the back yard and gather what wood he could find that wasn't wet. Once Reba and I heard you were on your way, we started heating water and toting it to the bathroom so you could have a bubble bath like I promised. Nothing like a nice hot bubble bath to lift your spirits."

"Gator prepared a bubble bath for me last night," Michelle said without thinking. The two elderly ladies exchanged hopeful looks. "He even helped me rinse my hair over the bathroom sink."

Gator cleared his throat and stood, uncomfortable with the silence that followed Michelle's declaration. "I'd better check things out in town and see what's going on," he said.

"You're coming back for dinner, aren't you?" Fiona asked. "I bought a grill yesterday. Reba helped me put it together. I also bought chicken breasts. I figured you could fire up the grill and cook them for us."

"I don't think so, Mom," he said. "I really need to

help in town since I've been MIA the last two days." Gator knew he was making excuses, but he'd spent too much time with Michelle already. He couldn't look at her without thinking how they'd spent the last couple of days and nights; and for the first time in his life he'd been getting butterflies in his stomach. It was time for him to back off because he knew Michelle was going to find a way to get back to Baton Rouge no matter what.

"But son, you have to come," Fiona said. "I don't know the first thing about cooking on a barbecue grill."

"That's right," Reba said, joining in. "We're going to need all the help we can get."

Gator felt himself weakening. "I guess I can come back for a little while," he said hesitantly, at the same time wondering if his mom even suspected that she was putting him in an awkward position. He could feel Michelle's eyes on him. Hell, she probably figured he owed it to her to hang around while she was in town. He'd never met a woman yet who didn't get possessive once things turned intimate. "But I can't stay long," he added quickly. Maybe he'd drop by the Night Life Lounge and see if his buddy needed any help getting the place on its feet again.

He bade the three farewell and bounded down the porch toward his truck. He disappeared a moment later in a cloud of red dust.

Michelle watched him go, feeling a heaviness inside. He seemed in a big hurry to leave. Not that she was surprised. Gator Landry was running scared.

#

"Now, dear, how about that bath?" Fiona asked, putting her arms around Michelle's shoulders. "You know, I feel as if I've known you all my life. Reba has told me so much about you."

Chatting easily with the woman, Michelle followed her inside the house and to the bathroom, where a tub waited, partially filled with scented water. Her mind instantly replayed images of the tub Gator had prepared for her, of the two of them sitting next to her on the couch wearing only a bathrobe that showed off his powerful thighs and calves, of Gator leaning over her, his hair-roughened body brushing against hers.

"You shouldn't have gone to so much trouble," Michelle told the woman, trying to get a grip on her thoughts, "but I certainly appreciate it."

Fiona reached into a cabinet and pulled out a fluffy towel and washcloth, as well as a new bar of soap. "Reba bought this specialty soap for you yesterday," she said, handing Michelle the items. "She figured you would like the smell."

Michelle sniffed the soap and gave a huge sigh. "It's heavenly," she said, touched that the two had gone to so much trouble for her. "I only have one request. Do you have any hair clips? I'd like to put my hair up so it doesn't get wet."

Fiona smiled. "I'll bet I do. Just give me a few minutes to look for them." She returned right away. "Will these work?" she asked, holding a handful of large hairpins.

"Perfect," Michelle said. "Thank you."

The woman smiled. "Now you enjoy your bath. I'll look around and see if I can find something for you to wear. I think I'm a size larger than you, but we can make do for the time being."

Michelle emerged from the bathroom half an hour later wearing one of Fiona's dresses, a simple blue cotton shift. The fit wasn't bad although it was a bit on the short side, but the sandals Fiona had lent her were too wide for her feet. Michelle kicked them off and decided to go barefoot. She braided her hair and coiled it at the back of her head, using Fiona's hair clips to hold it in place.

"Now if I only had my makeup," Michelle said laughingly as the women applauded her appearance. "I feel naked without it."

"Makeup?" Fiona asked, raising two brows. She stood and motioned for Michelle to follow her into her bedroom. She opened a drawer and presented her with an old cigar box.

"I only wear makeup if I'm going out which is mostly to church. You're welcome to it."

Michelle glanced inside the box and, much to her satisfaction, found several items she could use. "Thank you," she said. "I'll put the box back when I'm finished." Fiona left her with it, and Michelle applied the makeup, using the mirror over the bathroom sink. Once she was satisfied, she returned the cigar box to the drawer and reentered the kitchen. Both Reba and Fiona complimented her, and Michelle smiled, thankful for the bath and the makeup.

She rubbed her hands together. "Now, what can I do to help?"

"You can join us at the table and give me a full report on the damage to my house," Reba said. "I didn't want to question Gator."

Michelle took the chair beside her grandmother. Fiona put another glass of iced tea in front of her as Michelle told Reba what all she and Gator had managed to get done, as well as what was left to do. "It would be best if you could hire one of those companies to come out and put industrial-sized fans on the first floor and stairs; otherwise it's going to take the downstairs longer to dry and might cause your furniture to mildew."

Reba nodded. "That sounds like a good idea."

Michelle took a sip of tea. "Gator managed to gather most of the debris in the yard. He stacked it into several piles. You will probably want to have it hauled off. Also, as you know, a number of windows were broken in the storm. I think I managed to get most of the glass up. We covered the broken ones with plastic."

"Oh, thank goodness," Reba said. "The power company is working around-the-clock since so many folks are without electricity, but I have no idea how long it will take them to get my power restored since I'm so far out in the boonies."

"That's why you're going to stay with me until everything is taken care of," Fiona said. "As for your cats—"

"The cats will be fine," Michelle said, interrupting. "Gator has promised to see to them." She gave her grandmother a stern look. "Sorry to change the subject, but after this incident, I insist that you get a telephone, as well as wear one of those accident alert buttons on your wrist or hang around your neck."

Reba sighed. "I suppose, at least for the phone. Besides, Fiona showed me how much I miss having folks to talk to. I just didn't want much to do with people after your grandfather died."

"He died a very long time ago, Grand," Michelle said.

"I know. But sometimes it seems like yesterday." She gave another sigh. "I suppose it's time I moved on, as you young people like to say."

They talked for a while longer, and then Fiona took Michelle on a tour of the house. Everything was as cheery as the kitchen, decorated in splashes of yellow and white. Crisp white curtains billowed at the windows and thriving plants adorned every available table and shelf. Fiona opened the door to Gator's old bedroom, and Michelle stepped inside.

What surprised her most was the number of books in the room. One wall had been devoted entirely to book cases, upon which rested a variety of paperbacks, ranging from mystery and detective stories to horror novels. Interspersed among them was an odd assortment—books on reptiles and fish, and extrasensory perception.

"Matthieu loved to read as a child," Fiona said. "He wasn't crazy about his schoolbooks, but the boy must've read every mystery ever written. He was a bit of a loner, I reckon. Never had any real close friends."

Michelle nodded, taking in the old retro record player and albums that lined another shelf, and a tall stack of CDs. She thumbed through his CD collection, finding country-western, hard rock, alternative, and a couple of gospel albums. She felt like a snoop, but she was hoping his personal things would offer some insight into the man. They didn't. The real Gator Landry was neatly tucked inside the man, and she doubted if he'd ever let anyone really see him. She glanced up at the twin bed with its old-fashioned quilt that she knew Fiona had made. Over the bed hung a simple wooden crucifix, its polished surface glinting in the afternoon sun.

"Matthieu was such a neat boy," Fiona said, absently straightening a picture on the wall. "His father was very particular. Everything had to be in its place." She chuckled. "I'm afraid I've grown a bit lax since his death."

"Your home looks great to me," Michelle said.

"I'd rather be working in my garden or the flower beds," the woman confessed. She smiled suddenly. "Come outside and see my flowers. Or should I say what's left of them since the storm."

For the next half hour, while Reba dozed on the front porch, Michelle followed Fiona over the grounds as the woman pointed out various flowers and shrubs she'd planted and nurtured over the years. "It will take a lot of work getting them in shape again after all the damage done to them."

Michelle was amused as Fiona rattled off the history of each plant as if it were a member of the family. They ended up spending the better part of the afternoon working in the flower beds, digging holes and replanting a number of flowers and shrubs that had been ripped from the ground. They tied back Fiona's prized rosebushes that had been particularly damaged in the storm. Michelle found several strips of wood in the garage and tucked them inside the bushes, adding more ties for additional support.

"You're pretty good at this," Fiona said once

they'd done all they could for the roses.

Michelle smiled. "I used to help Grand with her gardening when I spent the summers with her. I've always loved flowers. I must have two dozen house plants at home."

Fiona nodded. "You're probably in a hurry to get back."

Michelle nodded. "My job is very important to me," she said.

"Everyone needs something meaningful in their life," Fiona replied. "I don't know what I'd do without my flowers and my church work." She paused. "But I think a family is important too, don't you?"

Michelle thought it an odd question. "If you meet the right person," she said. "Unfortunately, I haven't had much luck in that area." She wondered, even as she said it, why it was so easy to talk to Fiona.

"Maybe you aren't looking hard enough."

Michelle laughed at the serious expression on Fiona's face. "I'm not advertising at online dating services, if that's what you mean. But most men, wherever you meet them, don't seem to have a sincere interest in marriage and family these days."

Fiona smiled and plucked a perfect rosebud that had miraculously survived the storm. She handed it to Michelle. "Men are a lot like roses, dear. They each have their share of thorns that make it tough to get close to them. And their hearts are just as delicate and fragile as a rose petal, believe it or not. But with the right amount of love and nurturing and understanding, they too can blossom into something wonderful."

Michelle gazed at the rose thoughtfully. "What a lovely comparison, Fiona. You should write poetry."

The woman laughed and waved the statement aside. "You look tired, dear," she said to Michelle after a while. "Why don't you rest now?"

It sounded like a great idea to Michelle. "I think I'll lie on that chaise lounge in the shade," she said. "Unless there's something else I can do to help you."

"Go ahead," Fiona said, shooing her in that direction. "You've done enough work."

Michelle pulled off her work gloves and handed them to Fiona. Still clutching the rose bud between her fingers, she crossed the backyard to the lounge chair that sat beneath a giant oak. She adjusted the back into a reclining position and lay down, crossing her long legs at the ankles.

So peaceful, she thought, hearing the screen door close behind Fiona as the woman went back into the house. A breeze rustled the leaves overhead and fanned her cheek. She closed her eyes. She wasn't surprised when Gator's face came into view, and she wondered if she would ever be able to close her eyes without seeing him.

#

Gator made his way across the backyard toward the garage where his mother claimed he would find the new barbecue grill. He came to a screeching halt when he spotted Michelle sleeping in the chair. He stepped closer.

She looked clean and fresh in a blue summer dress, and her face was as delicate in sleep as the rose in her lap. Her hair had been pulled back, but some of it had escaped, and blond tendrils wafted over her face in the breeze. She had never looked lovelier. He slid his gaze downward to her slender legs and smiled at the sight of her bare feet. Her eyelashes fluttered open then, and she appeared surprised at finding him there.

"Did I fall asleep?"

He nodded. "Looks that way."

"Oh." She rose up and patted her hair self-consciously. "I must've been more tired than I thought."

Her words seemed to amuse him. "You didn't get much sleep last night, as I recall."

"That's true," she said. She wondered how long he'd been watching her. "When did you get here?"

"Just this minute. My mother sent me out to find the grill, with firm instructions not to wake you."

Michelle noticed he'd changed clothes. He looked good in a short-sleeve cotton print shirt and the usual blue jeans. "Is there anything I can do to help?”

He didn’t answer right away. “You could do one thing, Mic,” he said at last. “You could stop tempting me beyond rational thought. You could stop haunting my dreams at night. That would help a great deal.” With that he walked away.

Chapter Nine

Michelle couldn't remember the last time that chicken had tasted so good. Having spent the past few days eating hot dogs and canned tuna and Spam, the grilled chicken was a real treat. Fiona had picked some of the last of her vegetables from the garden and, of course, there was also the old standby these days, pork and beans from a can. Michelle took a serving out of politeness but decided she'd eaten enough pork and beans to last a lifetime.

Gator was surprisingly quiet over dinner, although he gave a progress report on the work in town. A group of Mennonites had arrived that afternoon with several truckloads of lumber and planned to work as long as necessary to get people back into their homes. Donations had already started pouring in, through both the Red Cross and from churches and private citizens trying to assist the homeless. An anonymous caller had donated a brand new mobile home for a family of six who'd lost their trailer when part of the mobile-home park had been destroyed. Gator and the town's officials hoped it would spark more donations, since FEMA was not giving out any trailers.

It was dark by the time they finished dinner, and while Michelle assisted the women in cleaning up, Gator lit the kerosene lamps. Michelle sensed the change in him. He was withdrawing. It was clear by the way he avoided eye contact with her, by the way he was careful not to stand too close, and by the way he walked clear around the table to avoid brushing past her. It irritated the daylights out of her. All her insecurities threatened to surface, but she forced them back. She was not going to let Gator's behavior upset her, she told herself. She did not deserve it. She had given him the best part of her. If he chose to back off, that was his problem.

It had been good between them—downright wonderful, as a matter of fact. Perhaps that was the problem. Maybe Gator realized he wasn't likely to find it so good anywhere else. Something had clicked between them, not only physically, but emotionally. She was certain Gator knew that. She had seen it in his eyes, felt it in his tender kiss, and heard it in his sighs of pleasure.

Gator could deny it all he wanted, but deep down he had to recognize it for what it was—love. Still, she would bite off her tongue before she'd try to convince him. She would never push or try to extract promises from him. Heaven knew, she'd had enough of that from her parents, always vying for their attention, living on false promises, playing second fiddle to their busy careers and social life.

It hadn't been much better with Jeffrey. With him, medicine and his patients had come first. All his energies had been geared to that cause, and by the time he could schedule an evening with her, he was emotionally drained. She had not minded at first, so impressed was she with his dedication to others. But now she realized he'd spent a great deal of time whining to her about it afterward or breaking dates simply because he was too exhausted to do anything. And she had been exhausted too, having worked right alongside him. Yet, somehow that fact had escaped him. She had been shortchanged in the relationship. She didn't feel sorry for herself any longer, thank heavens, but she was determined not to let it happen again. From now on, she would get back what she gave to a man. She would come first in his life or not at all.

"Why don't we sit on the front porch for a bit?" Fiona suggested, interrupting Michelle's thoughts. The older woman untied her cotton apron and folded it. "It's much cooler."

Gator had a refusal formed on his lips but bit it back. He couldn't very well rush off without appearing rude. He would stay ten or fifteen minutes, then excuse himself, saying he had to get back to town. He knew it was crazy to stay. He hadn't been able to keep his eyes off Michelle all evening, and every time she caught him staring he glanced away. He felt like a teenager again, trying to catch her scent as she passed by him. He would have half the town laughing at him behind his back by the time she returned home.

Reba and Fiona carried the conversation for a while; then, as though perfectly synchronized, they stood and excused themselves, announcing they were ready for bed. The screen door slammed closed behind them, and Gator suddenly found himself alone with Michelle.

He gazed at her for a moment, tracing her silhouette in the moonlight. Her neck looked long and sleek with her hair pulled back. He was tempted to loosen her hair from the braid affixed at the back of her head so he could watch her blond hair fall to her shoulders. His gut tightened at the thought of how she'd looked in bed with her hair fanning the pillow.

He should tell her how he was feeling, he thought. Tell her why he had to put some distance between them. It wasn't fair just leaving her hanging as he'd done with other women so many times before. This wasn't just any woman; this was Michelle, the girl he'd dreamed about for sixteen years. He owed her the truth. But before he could say anything, she stood and stretched.

"I think I'll turn in now," she said, giving him an easy smile. "I need to be up early in the morning and get into town. I want to see what can be done about my car." She patted Gator on the shoulder as she passed, much as she would have a brother or an old school buddy. She didn't see his look of surprise. "Good night," she said. And then she was gone.

For a moment, Gator merely sat there, staring at the chair she'd occupied only a moment before. He had planned his exit so carefully, rehearsed exactly what he'd say if she tried to pressure him or stop him from leaving. Oddly enough, she hadn't asked him about the future, nor had she made any reference to the time they'd spent alone at Reba's place. He hadn't had to lie or make excuses or offer his usual speeches.

And, frankly, he didn't quite know what to make of it.

Gator pushed himself up from the rocker and headed toward his truck, a frown drawing his brows together. He drove toward town, passing the Night Life Lounge, where a dozen or so cars were parked out front. Knowing the owner as he did, Gator figured the man would have iced down a couple of cases and was serving by candlelight. He braked, thinking he might stop by for a cold one and a bit of conversation.

He pulled off the road and sat in the parking lot for a full five minutes, trying to decide what to do. Well, why not go inside and pop a can, he thought. He was off duty and had put in a rough day. He deserved to kick up his feet and relax a bit. Of course, he would be expected to flirt and carry on with the women as he usually did. He hadn't let a sheriff's badge change him in that department.

But he had changed in other ways, he knew. He had fallen in love with Michelle Thurston all over again, and he was half-afraid someone would discover it, either in his face or in the way he talked. And how would he carry on an intelligent conversation, for Pete's sake? It was like she had stolen his mind. He couldn't think straight these days, and he hadn't had a decent night's sleep since Michelle had hit town. Boy, falling in love really took it out of a guy, he decided.

Once again, he told himself he had to get her out of town. Until then, he would have to put his partying aside. He didn't need a beer when he was confused to begin with. And he didn't need loud music or conversation when his thoughts were so jumbled he couldn't see his hands in front of his face.

Gator accelerated, pulling out of the parking lot and leaving the lounge behind, and he silently cursed the green-eyed woman who'd reduced him to such a sad state.

#

When Gator carried a bag of ice out to his mother's the following afternoon, he learned that Michelle had gotten up early and driven Fiona's car into town. She returned just as he was about to leave, her expression almost forlorn.

"Did you find someone to help you with your car?" he asked as she climbed out of his mother's old station wagon.

"They can't get to it until next week," she said. "It's going to take them a few more days to repair the bridge. Needless to say, they can't get to my car until the bridge is safe to cross. Then I have to wait my turn. My car was not the only one damaged in the storm," she added with a dejected sigh.

Gator crossed his arms and leaned against his truck. He couldn't help feeling a little sorry for her. She was wearing the same blue dress from the day before, her hair pulled into a demure ponytail, making her appear years younger. He realized then just how disappointed he'd been when he'd arrived and found her gone.

He hadn't slept worth a damn the night before, tossing and turning in his bed until the wee hours of the morning, his thoughts, as always, trained on Michelle. He wondered if she guessed what he was going through, the emptiness that stole over him when she wasn't around, the fear and frustration of seeing her and knowing nothing could come of their relationship. He wondered if she was going through any of it herself, but decided she probably wasn't. She was in such an all-fired hurry to get back home she probably had no idea how much he was suffering.

On one hand, he wanted her so badly he couldn't stand it. He wanted to feel her beneath him, opening herself up to him, just as his mother's roses opened their petals to receive the sun. He wanted to fill her with his own heat. He wanted to slip his tongue between those dewy lips of hers, hear her sigh of pleasure at his ear, feel her body tremble at his touch, and listen to the tiny gasping sound she made each time she climaxed. He wanted to reach out in his sleep and find her there, soft and warm and smelling like a piece of heaven. Once again, he chided himself for having such dangerous thoughts.

It irritated the hell out of him that he could wallow in indecision and utter bewilderment while she couldn't wait to get back to her life in Baton Rouge, to the doctor in his spiffy white lab coat and prestigious lifestyle. She might say the relationship was over, but he wondered if she wasn't waiting to see what happened with regard to the marriage between the man and his pregnant wife.

Gator had decided the night before to hand in his resignation at the end of the week. That in itself would take a big load off his mind, and by then the townspeople would at least be headed in the right direction. Although it could still be a couple of weeks before power was restored, at least the people of Temptation would have the necessities. What more could they expect from him?

But there was still the problem of what to do about Michelle. She was a constant distraction. With her out of the way, his life could return to normal. He could gear his thoughts in the right direction once more. He hadn't spent ten years of his life sweating his butt off in the sugar cane fields only to end up just like his father, chasing poachers through the swamps, busting up barroom brawls, risking his neck every time a husband and wife got into a heated argument. For the first time in his life he had money to travel, money to invest in something lucrative. He could go places and do things he'd never dreamed of before. He could be somebody, despite having lived with a man much of his life who had claimed he'd never amount to anything. But first, he had to put Michelle out of his life, this time for good.

"I'll take you home, Mic," he finally said, surprising himself as much as her with his words. But he'd already promised to help her. It was the least he could do.

"You?"

He nodded. "It might take a couple of weeks for someone to get to your car." He knew she'd never be able to wait. "Could you manage without it for a while?"

She shrugged. "I wish I had thought to take pictures of it with my cell phone," she said. "I could probably have gotten a loaner car. Who knows, I may still be able to. In the meantime, I can probably catch a ride to work with one of the other nurses, or, if need be, take a taxi."

"I'm sure you'll find someone to give you a lift," he said, wondering whether her doctor friend would be the one to accommodate her. "You'll have to come back for your car later."

Michelle pondered his offer. The man was obviously in a hurry to get rid of her, if he was willing to drive her all the way back to Baton Rouge personally. "When can you take me?" she asked.

Gator shoved his hands in his pockets. She'd jumped at the offer, just as he'd known she would. "I've got some things to take care of in town this afternoon, but I can drive you back tonight if you like. You'll probably need to make arrangements with a mechanic before you leave. I highly recommend Barnes Automotive."

Michelle stiffened. The guy wasn't wasting any time getting her out of town. It hurt knowing how anxious he was to see her go, especially after what they'd shared, but she'd be damned if she'd let him know. She smiled brightly. "Thanks, Gator. I'll be ready."

#

Gator picked Michelle up shortly before six o'clock that evening. She was waiting for him on the front porch, dressed in what looked to be new blue jeans and a crisp white cotton blouse that made her look as fresh as morning sunshine. She must have purchased them while she was in town. The jeans hugged her hips nicely and emphasized her trim waist and long legs. He felt his gut tighten when she leaned over to kiss Reba and his mother good-bye, after promising to return for her car in a week or so. Gator planned to be long gone by then.

"Ready?" he asked when she turned to him.

Michelle nodded and grabbed her purse. A moment later, they were on their way down the dirt road.

#

Reba and Fiona didn't speak at first. Finally, Reba turned to the other woman. "What d'you think, Fi? My granddaughter sure was in a hurry to get back. That can't be a good sign."

"I don't know what to think," Fiona said, shaking her head sadly. "All I know is my son is head over heels in love with that girl. He's so much in love, he can't see straight."

"Well, that's good isn't it?" Reba asked.

"Maybe, but they walked away from each other

before, y'know."

Reba waved the statement aside. "She was only sixteen years old at the time, too young to do anything about it."

Fiona sighed, looking tired and sad. "I have a feeling if they walk away from each other again, it'll be for the last time. And my son is just stubborn and hardheaded enough to do something like that."

#

Gator glanced at Michelle as he drove, wondering why she was so quiet. She was certainly different from most women he knew, who talked nonstop about things that didn't interest him in the least. "Are those new clothes you're wearing?" he asked.

She smiled. "Yes, your mother called a friend of hers who owns one of the dress shops in town, and the lady opened so I could come in and buy something." She laughed. "It's nice to finally wear clothes that fit."

He wanted to tell her she'd look good in a flour sack six sizes too big, but he didn't. "I'm glad she was able to help," he said instead.

"Your mother is very nice. I like her a lot." Gator gripped the steering wheel. Wasn't that just like a woman, he told himself. First, she worked on getting a man's mother to like her, and then she went after the man with both barrels.

"I'm really pleased your mother and my

grandmother hit it off so well," she said. "I worry about Grand out on the bayou all alone. At least she'll have a friend to check on her now and then. And your mother convinced her once and for all to have a telephone installed. I can't tell you what a relief that was."

Gator frowned. For a moment it sounded as if Michelle's relationship with his mother had absolutely nothing to do with him.

They rode in silence for more than an hour. Michelle nodded off and woke with a start when her head fell to the side.

"Tired?" he asked.

She smiled drowsily. "Riding always makes me sleepy; except when I drive, of course." She yawned wide.

"You can lay your head on my lap and stretch out on the seat If you like."

"That's okay." She yawned again.

"What's the big deal? You look as if you could use some shut-eye. I won't bite."

She blushed. "I know that. I just don't—" She paused.

"Don't what?"

"Don't want you to get the wrong idea."

So she was backing off, he told himself, surprised at the fact. Most women would have used the opportunity to cozy up to him, used their feminine wiles to get what they wanted from him. But

Michelle wasn't like most women, he'd learned over the past few days. Or maybe he'd known that sixteen years ago. Even then, she'd stood out among the crowd. Still, he couldn't stand to see her uncomfortable, with her head lopping to the side every time she dozed. He hated the position they were in. They'd gone too far to simply be friends.

"Look, Mic," he said, his dark eyes locking with hers briefly. "I've seen and tasted every inch of you. I don't think it would be out of line for you to lay your head on my lap."

Michelle blushed. He really knew how to put things into perspective and make her toes curl at the same time with his blatant remarks. Arguing with the man was pointless, and the fact that she couldn't stop yawning would only prove how sleepy she was and make him think she was afraid of touching him. How could she appear cool and indifferent to him if she acted afraid of his closeness? "Well, if you're sure," she finally said. "I just don't want to get in the way of your driving." She rearranged herself in the seat, and Gator raised his elbow so she could slip her head onto his lap.

That was his first mistake; Gator realized the moment her head came in contact with his thigh. He flinched inwardly when her ear brushed his crotch as she attempted to get comfortable. He gripped the steering wheel until his knuckles turned white.

Michelle tried to find comfort against Gator's hard thigh, but she was very much aware of his belt buckle at the back of her head, his zipper pressing against her hair. Her thoughts ran wild. She closed her eyes and tried to block out the sensual images. Thankfully, the sound of the engine and the slight rocking sensations of the truck made her sleepy.

It was all Gator could do to keep his eyes on the road ahead and not stare at the woman who slept with her head on his lap. He tried counting the exit signs, read billboards, and played a game of solitary cow poker whenever he spotted cattle grazing along the way. Nothing helped. The truck jostled her head slightly from time to time, creating enough friction to keep him thoroughly aroused. His mind ran amok. He imagined her waking, unbuckling his belt, working the zipper open ... He clenched his teeth.

Michelle awoke with a start when her head bumped the steering wheel, and the truck veered sharply to the right. She grabbed Gator's knee to keep from sliding off the seat and heard him groan.

"What are you doing?" she asked, raising up from his lap and rubbing the sleep from her eyes.

Gator didn't quite meet the look in her eyes. "We're stopping for dinner. There's a great steak restaurant at this exit," he said. "I promised you a steak dinner, remember?"

"Steak?" She said the word as though it were

foreign to her.

"Uh-huh." He drove up the ramp and paused at the stop sign.

"With a baked potato swimming in butter and sour cream and sprinkled with green onions and bacon bits?" she asked hopefully.

Gator was so happy to have her head off his lap, he grinned. "Yep, you can have anything you want."

#

Sharing dinner with Michelle was about as sensual as sharing her bed, Gator decided once their food arrived. He watched her, slightly amused, as she slathered enough sour cream on her potato to feed a family of four. She took great delight in swirling it about, mixing it with the creamy butter, bacon bits, onions, and shredded cheese. Once she'd popped a forkful into her mouth, she leaned back in her chair and closed her eyes dreamily. She attacked her T-bone with a vengeance.

Gator chuckled. "Do you always eat like there's no tomorrow?"

She smiled. "Only when I'm forced to live on canned food for a while." She ended up eating everything on her plate and some of his.

"I'm going to have to carry you out to my truck," Gator said, laughingly, once he'd paid the bill.

"Oh, Lord, I'm waddling like a duck," she exclaimed, following him out the door to the parking lot. "I'll have to eat salads and skip dessert for weeks to make up for cheating on my diet like this."

"You could always eat canned tuna," he said. "That's good for diets."

Michelle stopped dead in the middle of the parking lot and threw her hand over her mouth. "Did you have to mention canned tuna?" came her muffled reply.

They reached her apartment shortly after nine o'clock, the day having faded into night. Gator shut off the engine and stared straight ahead at nothing in particular. This was it, he thought. He'd done everything in his power to get her home, and now he didn't know what to do. He wasn't quite ready to let her go.

"Please come in for coffee," she said. "I can't just let you turn around and drive all the way back without a good dose of caffeine."

He pondered her offer. He really should get back, he told himself. There was a lot of work still left to do before he handed over his badge in a few days. But he couldn't say good-bye that easily to a woman who meant so much to him, to the woman he'd fallen in love with. Not only that, but he was curious. He wanted to see the inside of her apartment, find out how she lived.

"Maybe for a minute," he said at last. "But then I really do have to get back."

Chapter Ten

Gator liked her place, although it was a bit prissy for his tastes, with its overstuffed blue and yellow floral sofa and two solid blue chairs. On her coffee table sat a vase of flowers, the petals brown and shriveled. Gator wondered who had sent them to her, but there was no card so he had no way of knowing for certain. He wondered if they were from her doctor pal. Just thinking about it left a bad taste in his mouth.

Her kitchen was as warm and cheerful as his mother's, with brightly painted wicker baskets adorning one wall and another devoted to gleaming copper cookware. Michelle dumped the dead flowers and went about making coffee.

"Why don't you have a seat in the living room?" she suggested. "It won't take but a minute for the coffee to drip through."

Gator sank onto the fat sofa and leaned back, then kicked off his boots and propped his feet on the coffee table. He thought better of it after a moment and pulled them back down.

"You can put your feet up," Michelle said, watching him with a smile from the kitchen doorway.

"Thanks. My legs are kind of cramped from riding." He stretched them on the table once more, careful not to disturb the neat stacks of magazines and brass knickknacks.

"It sure is nice to have electricity and running water again," Michelle said a few minutes later as she carried in two cups of steaming coffee. "I should have asked Grand to come back with me."

Gator chuckled. "She wouldn't have left het pets or the bayou. It's in her blood."

"But not in yours, right?" Michelle said, offering him a dainty porcelain cup that looked much too small for his big hands. She wished now she had grabbed one of the old mugs she normally used. She took a seat in the chair across from him.

"Right," he said. With great amusement, Gator studied the cup she'd handed him. He was almost afraid it would crumble in his hands. He thought of the chipped pieces he'd served coffee to her in at his place and was almost embarrassed. He probably should put more thought into his possessions, he told himself, then realized how useless they were for a man bent on shucking anything that slowed or tied him down.

"So, have you decided where you'll go when you leave Temptation?" she asked.

He shrugged. "Who knows? I think I'll just travel for a while."

"I've always wanted to travel. I'd like to see Paris one day, but that's where everybody goes so maybe I should choose a different place."

"You could always come with me." Gator could not believe the words that had come out of his mouth.

Michelle didn't know whether he was serious or not, so she laughed to hide her uncertainty. "I have a job, remember? Plus, I'm afraid to leave the country because of my grandmother. I've always worried that something might happen and I wouldn't be able to get back quickly enough."

"What about your parents?"

"The truth? I can't count on them. I've never been able to count on them." She took a sip of her coffee. "Sorry. I don't mean to complain."

It occurred to Gator that Michelle had never discussed her parents, and he had not thought to ask. "You're not close to them?"

"I was raised by nannies. The only family I really had was Grand. My parents allowed me to spend the summers with her, but I think it had more to do with knowing I would look after her."

"That sucks."

"Yeah."

Their gazes met and locked, but neither of them said anything for a moment. “It’s none of my business,” Gator said, “but I think I would sit them down and tell them to take more responsibility. It’s not fair for you to give up part of your life just because it’s convenient for them.” He paused and shrugged. “But, hey, what do I know.”

“Gator?” Michelle set her cup down.

“Yeah?”

“I hope you find what you’re looking for.”

He set his cup down, pulled his legs from the table, and stuffed his feet into his boots, taking great pains with the simple task to keep from looking at her. “I hope you do too, Mic,” he finally said. He stood and shoved his hands in his pockets, not really knowing what to say or do. “I really have to go,” he said at last.

“I know.” Michelle rose from her chair. “And I have to go to bed because I’m working the morning shift.” She walked him to the door. She hesitated a moment before she reached for one of his hands and squeezed it. “I can’t begin to thank you enough for all you’ve done. I don’t know anyone who would have given so much time and effort and hard work—”

“I’m glad I could help, Mic,” he said, interrupting because she was embarrassing him. He raised her hand to his lips and kissed her palm, and she stroked his cheek.

The simple gesture surprised him as much as it touched him. He pulled her into his arms. “Aw, Mic,” he said before capturing her lips with his.

The kiss was long and deep and hungry, and Gator knew he’d been waiting to do just that all day. He wrapped his arms around her and pulled her close, enjoying the feel of her soft body against his. He caught her scent, tasted the inside of her mouth, and it was more than he could stand. “I want you, Mic,” he whispered against her mouth when he broke the kiss. “And as hard as I’ve tried, I can’t stop wanting you.”

She nodded. “I know.”

Without warning, he lifted her high in his arms and carried her down a short hall and through an open door. He caught a glimpse of a bed draped in soft pastels and ruffles and satin throw pillows trimmed in lace. Still holding Michelle, he quickly grabbed a handful of fabric and yanked hard, stripping it from the bed.

Michelle gave a throaty laugh as they fell onto the mattress together, arms and legs entwined. “You don’t like my taste in bed linens?” she asked, amused.

Gator began unbuttoning her shirt. “It’s a bit fussy.”

As soon as they were naked, Gator captured Michelle’s face in his hands and kissed her deeply. He did not take his time as he usually did, and

Michelle, trying to follow his lead, was as unrestrained as him. She wondered if it was Gator's way of saying goodbye, of wanting to leave her with a memory of him that she was not likely to forget. They climaxed together.

He kissed her then, tenderly, stroking her bottom lip with his tongue, their warm breath uniting just as their bodies had a moment before. Michelle felt a lump in her throat.

Without a word, Gator rolled off of her, captured her in his arms, and pulled her close. He stroked her hair and stared at the ceiling long and hard, as though it held the answers to the questions bouncing around in his head. He wished things could be different, but Mic had built a life for herself that was very much unlike what he would choose for himself. He could not envision Michelle living on a houseboat or picking up and moving whenever the urge hit him. She belonged in a nice house with a perfectly manicured lawn and a husband who came home to her every night. She deserved babies and fresh flowers and a place to store her delicate treasures.

She deserved a better man than he could ever be.

For a long time they merely lay there, each of them caught up in their own thoughts. Finally, Michelle drifted off to sleep. She was vaguely aware when Gator climbed quietly from the bed and stepped into his clothes. She feigned sleep when he kissed her tenderly on her forehead, and she didn't budge when she heard the front door close behind him. She got up to lock it, only to find the key on the floor of her laminated entry, only inches from the door. Gator had locked the deadbolt from the other side and shoved the key beneath the door to her side. She picked it up and put it on the table next to the door where she normally kept it. Finally, she headed back to bed.

She lay in bed for more than an hour thinking about Gator. At sixteen, she had run away from him, fearing what might happen if she let down her guard. Later, she had fantasized what it would feel like to lie naked in his arms. She had lived the fantasy, and it had been even better than she could have imagined.

She reached for the alarm clock on her nightstand and mentally closed that chapter in her life.

#

Gator's mood was dark when he parked in front of the sheriff's office the following morning, having slept only a couple of hours the night before. He had arrived home after midnight and gone to bed with hopes of catching up on his sleep. It had proved fruitless. Every time he closed his eyes he saw Michelle's face.

His office was a hole in the wall, with two jail

cells and a couple of battered metal desks. He stepped inside and was surprised to find several kids sitting on the hard plastic chairs in the waiting area, none of them more than thirteen or fourteen years old. His deputy came to attention at the sight of him.

"You got visitors, Sheriff," he said.

"So I see." Gator regarded the group of boys with an obvious lack of interest. He recognized them. They were refugees from the pool hall he'd closed down. "What can I do for you?" he asked, going over to his desk and sitting down. He propped his legs up and waited as all three approached him.

"You're Sheriff Landry, ain't you?" one of them said.

"That's right."

"My name's Billy Wilcox. This here is Ted and Bart Johnston."

"I know who you are," Gator said curtly. "What do you want?"

"You closed down the pool hall."

"Yeah, I did."

Billy folded his arms over his chest. "Mind telling us why?"

"Because I felt like it." He did not bother to add that it was a roach-infested dump or that he knew the owner served under-aged teenagers. He didn't owe them or anybody else an explanation. "Any more questions?"

"Yeah," Billy said. "Mind telling us where we're supposed to go now without a pool hall?"

Gator shrugged. "Not my problem, kid."

Billy Wilcox's face reddened. "Look, we didn't touch your old lady. The guy responsible for messin' with the old people in this town is long gone now, moved up north. It ain't fair to punish the rest of us because of what he did."

Gator didn't know whether to believe him or not, and he was almost sorry to hear that his mother's attacker might have left town before he could get his hands on him. But it would explain why there hadn't been any recent robberies of the town's older citizens. "Thanks for the tip," Gator said. "Now, go on home because I'm busy."

"We want the pool hall reopened."

"No."

"We'll clean it up, get rid of the roaches."

Gator was clearly surprised. He studied the boy for a moment, thinking he was kind of gutsy for coming in to talk to him. He could almost see himself in those defiant eyes, the stubborn tilt of the chin. "Then what? Go back to drinking when you're not anywhere close to twenty-one? I don't have time to mess with you kids."

"You could always get one or two of your deputies to come by from time to time to make sure nothing illegal is going on."

Gator scoffed at the idea. "My deputies and I are

not babysitters. Besides—" He paused. "I'm officially resigning in a few days. You'll have to wait and talk to the new sheriff."

The boy grunted. "It figures. Folks said you'd never stay. They said you would never be the man your daddy was."

One of the younger boys stepped forward. "Nobody cares about this town, and they sure don't care about us. There ain't nothing to do. My mama said that's why so many girls get into trouble."

"Is that so?" Gator said. "Well, you can tell your mama that the reason so many girls get pregnant is because they don't take precautions."

Billy Wilcox looked at his friends. "Let's go. We're wasting our time." He yanked open the door, and they filed out, one-by-one.

Gator's deputy shook his head. "Smart-aleck kid. Somebody needs to take a hickory switch to his hide and teach him some manners."

"I don't know," Gator said, staring at the door through which the boys had just exited. He felt as though he'd been kicked in the gut. "Maybe the kid knows what he's talking about."

#

Michelle eyed Jeffrey over the rim of her coffee cup as she sat across from him in the hospital cafeteria. He hadn't stopped whining and complaining since they'd taken their seats. Her head ached. They'd had bus-accident victims in early that morning, and they had just finished with the last patient. She'd been too tired to eat, so she'd taken only a cup of coffee from the line, hoping the caffeine would revive her.

"... I just can't take it anymore, Michelle," Jeffrey said, covering his eyes with one hand. "I don't know what I saw in the woman in the first place. All she does is cry and complain. Her ankles are swollen, she can't sleep at night, and she has indigestion all the time. It's driving me up the wall."

"Pregnant women are very emotional, Jeffrey," she said. "You'll just have to be patient."

"You wouldn't act like that, Michelle. You're always so cool and calm. You'd just accept it and try to make the best of it."

She offered him a wry smile. "Don't be too sure about that. I'll probably do my share of complaining when the time comes."

Jeffrey didn't seem to be listening. "I thought I'd go crazy while you were gone," he went on. "Please don't up and leave like that again without telling me."

Michelle frowned. Leave it to Jeffrey to forget a dangerous hurricane had sent her to Temptation, Louisiana, and that he had no right to expect her to get his approval before leaving town. She had been as patient with him as she could, but she was fast losing it.

"Listen up, Jeffrey," she said. "If you and your wife are having marital problems that's between the two of you and has nothing to do with me. I can't help you. Take her to dinner or a movie. Do something nice for her. You'd be surprised how far a little kindness goes."

"Yeah, right." His tone was sarcastic.

"You made the decision to marry her."

"I had no choice."

"Everybody has choices." Michelle was surprised by her own words. Now where had she heard that before? She ignored Jeffrey's hurt expression. "There is an opening in the OR," she said. "I've applied for the position."

He was clearly shocked. "Why didn't you tell me?"

"I only learned about it this morning. We didn't have time to chat once the bus-accident victims arrived."

"You just decided to leave the ER without discussing it with me first?"

"I saw no reason to discuss it."

He leaned forward. "But, Michelle, I need you in emergency. You're the best nurse I've got. How can you do this to me?" He sounded desperate.

Michelle was clearly surprised by his response. The man acted as though her decision was a personal attack against him, when, in fact, it had absolutely nothing to do with him. He obviously hadn't listened all those times she'd told him she needed a change, all those times she'd shared her goals with him. But then, he'd always been so wrapped up in his own problems, how could he have possibly heard?

"I'm sorry, Jeffrey, but I can't put my life on hold simply because you need a shoulder to cry on from time to time. Again, you should be talking to your wife, not me." She pushed her chair from the table and stood. "Now, if you'll excuse me, I think I'll get a sandwich before I head back to the ER. Would you care for anything?"

He looked like a child who'd just had his favorite toy taken from him. "No thanks. I've suddenly lost my appetite."

Michelle smiled and patted him on the shoulder. "It'll come back. And tomorrow you'll have a whole new set of problems to fret over." She hurried to the serving line, leaving him slumped in his chair.

#

Gator slammed the telephone down so hard that both deputies glanced up from their paperwork in surprise. One of them grinned.

"What's s'matter, still can't reach her?"

Gator shot him a dark look. "I don't know what you're talking about."

The deputy chuckled and ran one meaty hand over his balding head. "You ain't fooling nobody,

Sheriff. We all know you're chasing after some woman from Baton Rouge. What's the problem?"

Gator crossed his arms over his chest. He was making a fool out of himself over Michelle, just as he'd known he would. How could she have done this to him, reduced him to a sniveling, lovesick adolescent? She'd been gone one week now, and he was half crazy missing her. He was certain the whole town was having a good laugh over it, especially the folks at the Night Life Lounge, since he never stopped by anymore. Twice now he'd driven six blocks out of his way just to keep from passing it. If his friends found out he was going home every night to pine away over some woman, he'd never live it down.

"She's never home," Gator finally said. "That's the problem."

"Oh, so she's got a busy social life, eh?"

Gator shrugged. "I figure she's working. You know how nurses are, dedicated and all."

The deputy snickered, but swallowed his laughter when Gator glowered at him. "Yeah, you're probably right, Sheriff," he agreed.

"And she's involved in some youth program up there. It takes a lot of her time." Gator didn't know who he was trying to convince, his deputy or himself.

He shoved his chair from his desk and stood. He had no idea why he was trying to call Michelle in the first place. What would he say? As for her, he wondered if she would hang up on him.

He needed something to take his mind off her, he thought, until he made some decisions. Decisions that he should have made a week ago. Getting her out of town hadn't helped. All he did these days when he got off work was sit on the deck of his houseboat and stare off into space. His mother had asked him twice if he was coming down with something.

Every time he closed his eyes he saw Michelle as she'd looked the last time they had made love, and the way she'd pretended to be asleep when he left. She had not bothered to contact him because she was too proud, and because, unlike him, she had a full life. Why he ever thought she might try to fence him in was beyond him. She was more subtle. She would make it so damn good for a man that he couldn't stay away.

Damn woman! What did she think she was doing? She had no right to step into his life after sixteen years and turn it upside down and inside out. She had no right to make him fall head over heels in love with her.

"I'm leaving for the day," he said, rounding his desk, "and I don't want nobody to come looking for me." Gator slammed out the door a moment later, leaving the deputies grinning at their desks.

He drove for close to an hour, measuring the

town's progress as he went. He'd busted his butt over the past week; once again putting off his resignation when he saw how much there was still left to be done. It made him feel good in a way to know he had a hand in the recovery.

Gator pulled up alongside the brick building that used to house the pool hall. Pitiful-looking building, he thought. Nobody had ever tried to take care of it. The back door was torn completely off its hinges, a result of the storm, no doubt.

Gator stepped inside and squinted against the darkness. It was a big room, but about as shabby as they came. Heaven only knew when it had seen its last coat of paint. The pool tables were worthless, revealing rotting wood where they'd been stripped of their stained green felt. Somebody ought to do something about the place, he thought.

"What'cha doin' here, Sheriff?"

Gator almost jumped out of his skin at the sound of the voice. He turned quickly on his heels and saw someone sitting in the shadows. There was movement, and a second later, a young boy stepped into the light streaming in from a broken window. Gator recognized the boy who'd come into his office a week ago, Billy Wilcox.

Gator sighed his relief. "You sneak up on me like that again, and I'll lock you in the back of my patrol car," he said, although he was half smiling.

The boy smirked. "Aw, you ain't so tough,

Sheriff. Not as tough as my old man. He could whip your ass in a heartbeat."

"Watch your language, kid," Gator said. He studied the young face before him. "Did your daddy give you that black eye?" When the boy didn't answer, he went on. "Is that why you're hiding out here with the roaches?"

The boy looked partly embarrassed, partly scared. "Naw, I fell."

"Sure you did." Gator paused. "That's what I used to tell folks when my old man got rough with me," he said.

"Your daddy hit you?" Billy said in disbelief. "I thought he was supposed to be the greatest sheriff in the whole danged world."

"Yeah, that's what everybody thought." Gator looked around the room, then returned his attention to the boy. "I think I know your daddy. He hangs out at the Night Life Lounge. Drinks a little, huh?"

The boy gave a hoot of a laugh. "My old man ain't never drank a little of nothin'." His look sobered. "He don't like a damn thing I do. He says I ain't worth killin'." He touched the bruise lightly and winced. "Sometimes I think he'd like to do it personally."

"Yeah, well, that happens sometimes between fathers and sons. That doesn't mean you're bad. It just means your daddy doesn't know how to be a good father. Trust me, I know what I'm talking about. Besides, I think you're a pretty neat kid, and I don't particularly like kids, so that's a compliment."

"Why should I give a flip if you like me?"

Gator suppressed a smile. The kid was tough for his age. "'Cause you and I got a lot in common and 'cause I can get your old man off your back. If I feel like it," he added.

"What do I got to do in return?"

Gator crossed his arms over his chest and rocked back and forth on his heels. "Several things," he said. "You could check on my mother for me while I'm out of town. See that she has what she needs. Do some chores. And when I get back, you can be in charge of fixing up this dump." A look of incredulity passed over the boy's face. "I'll work on getting the money for it in the meantime." Gator had already decided he would go along with his plans for the town with or without the help of a bunch of tight-fisted politicians.

The boy didn't speak for a minute. In fact, he looked about ready to cry. "You can really get my old man off my back? How?"

Gator grinned. "All I have to do is talk to him, man-to-man. Is it a deal?" He held out his hand. He wondered for a moment if the boy would take it. When he didn't make a move to do so, Gator shrugged and started to pull it back. Without warning, the boy grasped his hand tightly and pumped it with more enthusiasm than Gator was prepared for.

"All right, Sheriff!" he said. "You got yourself a deal. Just tell me where your mother lives, and I'll be out there first thing tomorrow."

And then Gator knew the boy had not been responsible for hurting his mother, and that he'd probably told the truth about the real perpetrator leaving town. Gator had accomplished more than he'd expected.

#

Gator's business at the Night Life Lounge took less than five minutes. He called Billy Wilcox's father outside and shoved him hard against his truck. The man covered his face and begged Gator not to hit him.

"What's wrong with you, Wilcox? You scared to fight a man?" Gator ground out through tightly clenched lips. He knew a moment of rage that shook him to the core. He had to stay cool. He released the man, who fell to the ground.

"I ain't done nothin'!" Wilcox cried. "Why're you picking on me?"

"'Cause I don't like grown men beating up little boys, that's why." Gator reached for the man and dragged him to his feet. "I'm only going to give you one warning," he said, his tone menacing. "You lay another hand on that boy or anybody else for that matter, and I'm going to make you wish you'd never slid from your mama's womb. Do you understand what I telling you? I'm going to make you wish you had never been born."

The man nodded.

"And another thing; I'm going to be watching you. I better not catch you behind the wheel of your truck while you're all tanked up." Gator released him with such force, he sent the man sprawling to the ground. "I suggest you find yourself a job and get off the booze, old man, 'cause I'm not going to stop riding you till you do." Gator didn't wait for him to respond. He stalked over to his truck, got in, and drove away.

#

On Saturday morning Michelle awoke to the sound of steady knocking. Someone was at her door. She groaned and climbed out of bed, then, still half asleep, staggered toward the living room. She threw open the door and found herself face to face with Gator Landry. For a moment she was stunned into speechlessness.

"Damn, Mic, don't you even bother to find out who's on the other side of your door before you just open it?" Gator asked, stepping over the threshold. He kicked the door closed behind him. "Have you any idea how many women are raped and robbed and Lord only knows what else from doing just what you did?" He didn't wait for an answer. "How can you expect law enforcement to protect you when you open your door to anyone?"

She blinked. "Gator, what are you doing here? I know you didn't drive all this way to lecture me on home safety. Did you bring my car?"

"Your car's still sitting in line at the body shop. I told you they don't hurry things along in Temptation. Mind if I sit down?" He took a seat on the couch without waiting for permission. For a moment, all he could do was stare at her in her pink shorty pajamas that brought out the flush in her cheeks. Her hair was tousled about her face beguilingly, her eyes dreamy and sleep-filled. Her long legs held his attention.

"I tried to call you at least a half dozen times over the past week, Mic, but you weren't home." It had been more than a half dozen, but he wasn't about to fess up and lose bargaining power. He'd practiced his speech on the drive up, but now he felt unsure.

"I've been busy."

"Oh? You been pulling double shifts at the hospital?"

"No."

So she was going to play hardball, he thought. Make him work for his information. "Does this mean you're not going to tell me what you've been up to?"

Michelle planted her hands on her hips. Oh, the nerve of the man! Here he was questioning her, after he'd walked out on her. "Get this straight, Gator Landry," she said. "I don't sit home and wait for any man."

He couldn't help but grin at her show of temper. Damn, but she was cute. And sexy. And everything he'd ever wanted in a woman. "Not even for me, Mic?"

"Not even for you," she said firmly.

He rose slowly from the sofa and closed the distance between them. He stopped only inches from her, leveling his gaze at her green eyes. "I've been sitting home nights over you, love."

Michelle almost shivered at his husky tone. His voice caressed her; the heat in his eyes warmed her belly. "You don't really expect me to believe that, do you? What happened? Did the Night Life Lounge burn to the ground after I left?"

He chuckled and reached for her, but she took a step back. "I owe you an apology," he said.

"Damn right you do."

"I'm sorry."

She was taken off guard by the earnest look in his eyes. "You should be."

"I was scared, Mic. Terrified, in fact." He held out his hands as if surrendering. "I had to back away and clear my mind."

She felt herself softening against her will. "What

on earth could you be afraid of, Gator Landry?"

"Of falling in love with you, darlin'," he said simply. "But it's too late now because it happened, and there's not a blasted thing I can do about it. And now I realize I don't want to do anything about it. I just want to keep on loving you."

Michelle's knees suddenly felt about as sturdy as warm jelly. "What about all those grand plans you had of traveling all over the world?"

Gator shot her an amused look. "You're going to make me grovel, aren't you?" When she didn't answer, he went on. "Remember when I told you I never felt as though I belonged?" She nodded. "That's before I realized I belonged with you. Where I go or what I do really doesn't matter anymore as long as you're beside me."

"Maybe now, but what about next week?"

His look sobered. "I don't make decisions lightly, Mic. I wouldn't have come here if I hadn't thought this over very carefully. Hell, that's all I've been doing the past week." When she continued to look doubtful, he went on. "You're the only person who ever loved me for who I am. Besides my mother," he added with a chuckle, "but that's her job. And I know you love me, Mic." He smiled tenderly. "Before you came along I felt I wasn't worthy of love. I thought I was a nobody, and I was scared you'd find out just how much of a nobody I was if I let you get too close."

"Oh, Gator." She felt her heart swell with love for the man, knowing how hard it was for him to tell her such things about himself.

"I've never had a high opinion of myself. It's not important why, but I never felt I measured up. That's the real reason I didn't want to be sheriff. I was flattered when they asked me, but I was afraid I would let them down. I was afraid I couldn't be the man my daddy was. Now I realize I only have to be myself." He shrugged and gave her a lopsided grin. "I figure if you love me, I can't be too awful bad."

Michelle was clearly touched by the confession. "Does that mean you're going to keep the job?"

"I start law enforcement training on Monday."

She shook her head, stunned at the announcement. "I'm very proud of you, Gator."

She probably had no idea what those simple words meant to him. "I want you beside me, Mic," he said gently. "I'm here to offer you a job and a marriage proposal."

Michelle was clearly stunned by his words. "You are?"

Gator still felt unsure of himself. "Perhaps you'd like to discuss the job first. It's working with a youth group I'm putting together as soon as I can squeeze the money out of those tightwads in City Hall. Plus, the clinic could use a hand now and then."

She waved the statement aside. "I think I'd like

to hear about the marriage proposal first, if you don't mind."

He smiled, almost shyly. "I'd like for you to be my wife, Mic," he said, and held his breath waiting for her answer. "I'll understand if you need to think about it." She continued to look at him in utter stupefaction, so he continued. "I don't care where we live as long as you'll agree to spend a weekend on the houseboat with me every once in a while. And maybe do a little fishing with me. In return, we'll hire a contractor, and you can decide what kind of house you want him to build. I love you, Michelle. With all my heart," he added solemnly. He pulled the velvet box from his pocket and opened it.

All at once Michelle was in his arms, laughter bubbling from her throat. Gator grinned, slipped the ring on her finger, and then captured her laughter with his lips. "Does this mean yes?" he asked when he raised his head.

"Yes!" she squealed.

"And you'll wait for me while I'm in training?" Before she could answer, he added, "I'll be able to see you weekends, and it's only for six weeks. It'll give you time to decide if you're interested in working with these kids or helping out at the clinic in Temptation." He shrugged. "Or maybe you just want to lie around naked on my houseboat for a while and make babies. We have a lot of time to make up for, love."

She nodded, unable to take her eyes off his face. He looked radiant. "Sixteen years worth," she said. "I can't wait to get started."

He kissed her tenderly, fitting himself against the soft curves of her body. "I'm going to be a good husband, Mic. I swear."

"I know that, Gator. You're already a good man, you know."

"Don't ever stop telling me that, darlin'. And don't ever stop telling me how much you love me and need me. I don't think I'll ever get tired of hearing it." He kissed her again. And again, until their breaths were hot and raspy. Their groans of pleasure rose over their heads.

Michelle broke the kiss. "Shouldn't we tell your mother and my grandmother?"

He pondered her question. "Maybe we should wait and tell them in person. They won't be expecting it."

"It'll be a shock, I'm sure."

He nodded. "We'll break it to them gently."

Michelle anchored her hands around his neck. Gator grinned and swooped her up in his arms with very little trouble. "We've got time to tell them. But right now we're going to concentrate on making up for lost time. Maybe if we work hard ..."

Michelle snuggled against him as he carried her into the bedroom.

About the Author

Charlotte Hughes published her first category romance in 1987, a Bantam Books' *Loveswept,* titled *Too Many Husbands,* which immediately shot to #1 on the Waldenbooks Bestseller list. She went on to write almost thirty books before the line closed in 1998.

Although Charlotte is widely known for her laugh-out-loud romantic comedies, she went on to pen three Maggie Award-winning thrillers for Avon Books in the late nineties, before resuming her first love, funny stories about people falling in love. She thrilled readers with her hilarious books, *A New Attitude* and *Hot Shot,* the latter of which won the Waldenbooks Greatest Sales Growth Achievement in 2003.

Her books received so many accolades that she was invited to co-author the very popular Full House series with mega-star author Janet Evanovich.

With that series behind her, Charlotte began her own, starring psychologist Kate Holly; *What Looks Like Crazy, Nutcase, and High Anxiety,* creating a cast of somewhat kooky but always loveable and funny ensemble characters.

To keep current with Charlotte and her projects, please sign up for her Readers Group and get free excerpts as well as the latest news.

You can also visit her website at http://readcharlottehughes.com and follow her on Twitter @charlottehughes.

If you enjoyed *Welcome to Temptation* we think you will also enjoy *See Bride Run!* and *Tall, Dark, and Bad*, both released by Charlotte in 2014-2015, as well as her backlist. Her next book, *The Devil and Miss Goody-Two-Shoes,* tentatively scheduled for August, promises to be another fun read! The following is an excerpt from that book:

The Devil and Miss Goodie Two-Shoes

Chapter One (Excerpt)

Kane Stoddard cut the engine on his battered Harley, shoved the kickstand in place with the heel of his boot, and read the address on the rustic frame building once more. As he climbed off his bike, he could still feel the vibrations from the powerful engine rumbling through his body. His right hand ached from having gripped the throttle for so many hours. His shoulder muscles were sore. He didn't care. It felt good to use all the parts of his body again.

Prison had taught him to appreciate the simple things.

He sucked his breath in deeply and tasted the crisp Mississippi air. It was fresh and clean with no lingering scents of urine and disinfectant. Spring. How fitting to be given a new start in life when everything around him was coming alive as well.

He smiled, then realized it was the first time he'd smiled in months. Not that he'd had a whole lot to smile about these past three years. But, out of the blue, everything had changed. The warden had called him into his office to apologize for the terrible mistake they'd made, *they* being the judicial system that Kane had long ago lost respect for—the *same* system that put bank robbers behind bars for forty-five years and gave child molesters four.

"I've wonderful news for you, Mr. Stoddard," the warden of Leavenworth Prison had said, as if addressing inmates respectfully took the sting out of all the other humiliations they were forced to endure. "A man fitting your description robbed a Memphis convenience store a couple of months ago. The clerk shot him in the chest. The man eventually died but not before he confessed to several crimes, including the one for which you were convicted." The warden paused. "His story checked out, and his DNA was at the crime scene. He was able to give details.

The warden paused and took a deep breath. "So ... It appears you were wrongfully convicted."

Now, three days after his release from the Hot House—the name everyone gave to that notorious federal prison—Kane stood before Abercrombie Grocery. He thought of the bundle of letters in his duffel bag that had led him from Leavenworth to Hardeeville, Mississippi.

Melanie Abercrombie had begun writing to him a year earlier when she'd received his name from her pastor. Kane suspected the preacher hoped his congregation would bring a few criminals to salvation. Well, Miss Abercrombie hadn't saved his soul, but she'd certainly made the small Mississippi town and its occupants sound interesting. Through her letters, Kane knew the good Reverend Potts had a weakness for rhubarb pie, and his wife a fondness for gossip. He'd also read about the Babcock's, who owned the local bakery and often left their loaf bread and rolls on the shelves too long instead of moving them to the "thrift" section and marking them half-price. *This,* Miss Abercrombie declared, was probably due to the fact that their teenage daughter, Desiree, refused to buy her clothes at the moderately priced Aaronson's Department Store like everyone else, preferring the Neiman Marcus (Melanie had called it Needless Markup) in the new mall in the next town instead. It was no wonder folks in Hardeeville were being forced to pay top dollar for stale bread.

Kane had read each and every letter, sometimes three or four times before tucking them into the shoe box beneath his cot. He'd never answered them, of course, not only because he couldn't think of a damn thing to say to the woman but because he didn't want anyone to think the letters were important. The minute someone found out something mattered at Leavenworth they took it away.

Nevertheless, he had found himself wondering about Melanie Abercrombie: what she looked like, the sound of her voice. She had to have a pretty voice, because she'd mentioned singing in the church choir. As for looks, she was probably as plain as a dust mop, he'd convinced himself. Otherwise, she wouldn't spend all her free time writing to him.

Kane pulled his duffel bag from the bike and approached the store, trying to decide if it looked as Melanie Abercrombie had described it. The building had to be at least a hundred years old, the wood faded and warped in places from the weather. A vintage soda-pop machine shared space with two long benches on the front porch, where a faded green awning offered relief from the elements. Double screen doors marked the entrance, both of which sagged and looked as though they'd come completely unhinged in the next strong wind. Beside one door a small sign listed the hours of operation. A sign on the other side of the doors listed the rules. *No loitering, profanity, or alcoholic beverages allowed.* Kane didn't have to be psychic to know who'd put up the sign. Even in her letters, Miss Melanie Abercrombie had come across as a real Southern lady.

He paused before the door, suddenly nervous at the thought of meeting the woman who'd written to him faithfully the past year. How would she react when she saw him for the first time? His release had come about so quickly, he hadn't had a chance to notify her of his whim to visit.

#

Melanie Abercrombie was in a sour mood, brought on by hunger pangs, her younger sister's desperate, incessant phone calls, and a feeling of being overwhelmed. She peered through clunky square-framed glass at the mess before her.

Abercrombie Grocery was as disorganized and cluttered as a child's playroom, proof that her father preferred visiting with his customers and listening to gospel music to sweeping and restocking shelves. Mel ran a finger across the lid of a jar of pickled beets where a layer of dust covered the price.

She knew she was partially responsible for the mess. Her flower shop had been in an uproar for a solid month, what with three weddings and two high school proms. It was so bad her assistant, Eunice Jenkins, claimed she was getting varicose veins from standing on her feet so long, and prickly heat rash from sweating and handling pompoms. Mel simply hadn't had time to come by her father's store and clean the way she usually did. It was no wonder folks were driving into town to shop at the new Thrifty Sack.

Nevertheless, Mel had had no idea how bad business had been until she looked through her father's financial records. Only then did she realize they would have to take desperate measures. The store *must* be cleaned up once and for all. They'd have to pull up all that scarred linoleum and tear down the warped shelves. They'd have to patch the roof over the meat cooler and repair the faucet on the bathroom sink, and have someone look at the old heating and air conditioning unit that never quite kept the place warm enough in winter or cool enough in the summer.

Mel sighed heavily. It was going to take so much time and money, neither of which she had very much of these days.

That brought her to the next problem: Where the heck was the carpenter she'd hired to *do* the work? She groaned inwardly as she wondered about him. She'd hired the man sight unseen from a Craig's List ad stating he was unemployed and would work cheap as a handyman. She'd later learned, through the grapevine at church, that the fellow was unemployed due to a tendency to drink and forget about work altogether.

Mel was interrupted from her thoughts by the sound of a motorcycle pulling in front of the store. Less than a minute later, one of the screen doors was thrown open and a man stepped through.

"Melanie Abercrombie?" he asked, trying to make himself heard above a modern rendition of "Jesus Loves Me" coming from a radio at the back of the store.

At first all Mel could do was stare at him.

She felt her jaw drop clear to her collar as she

regarded the man before her. His head and face were covered with snarled blue-black hair. His eyes were just as black; his look hard, flat, and emotionless. It was the sort of face one expected to find on Wanted posters, the sort of face that prompted decent folks to lock their doors at night before they went to bed.

So *this* was her carpenter. No wonder he couldn't keep a job.

"Well, it's about time you got here," she said, her voice as crisp as fried salt pork. She wasn't going to allow herself to be put off by that beard. She took in his clothes, the blue sweat-stained work shirt and shamefully tight jeans. He looked tough, lean, and sinewy, and probably could do the work if he stayed sober. "I've been waiting for you all day."

"You have?" Kane was clearly surprised. He couldn't imagine how she'd learned he was getting out.

"Yes," she replied, noting he didn't look the least bit remorseful for being so late. Didn't he *want* the job, for heaven's sake? "I suppose an apology is out of the question," she said.

Kane's mind went blank. "You can apologize if you want, but I certainly don't expect it."

Her irritation flared. "I wasn't talking about *me* apologizing to *you,"* she said tightly.

His bafflement quickly turned to annoyance. She had obviously called the prison, although he couldn't imagine why. She had never once tried to contact him by phone. "Why should *I* apologize?" he asked. "I came as quickly as I could. Hell, I don't even have to be here."

"Oh, is that right?" she quipped, staring straight into his lethal black eyes. She paused. "You think I'm desperate, don't you?"

He was growing more confused. "Come again?"

"That's it, isn't it?" She fidgeted with the buttons on her blouse. "You think I need you so badly that I'll put up with this sort of behavior."

Kane was truly at a loss as he studied the woman before him and wondered where in the hell the conversation was going. "I don't think you're desperate," he said, at the same time wondering if she expected him to court her in return for all those letters. She was clearly not his type. Her skirt and blouse were too prim and proper; her hairstyle—slicked back into a bun—too severe. Her glasses were downright ugly and made her face appear misshapen. "I don't want to appear rude, Miss Abercrombie, but I'm not looking to get romantically involved with *anyone* right now. I'm just looking to make a fresh start."

"What?" Mel's head spun. What in blazes was he talking about? Did he think she was making a pass at him? Was he insane? She opened her mouth to speak, but he cut her off.

"Look, I don't want us to get off to a bad

beginning. I'm not sure I would have made it this past year without your letters." It wasn't easy for him to be so honest, but she had done much for his morale these twelve months; he owed her.

Mel was at a loss. He wasn't making sense. "Letters? What letters? Who *are* you?"

"Kane Stoddard."

She froze as realization swept through her with the force of a tidal wave. "Kane Stoddard? From Leavenworth Prison?" He nodded, and she thought she detected a small smile, but it was hard to tell with the beard.

"But how can that be?" she asked herself out loud. The Kane Stoddard she knew was a convicted killer, serving life without parole. How had he gotten out? The answer came to her with lightning-quick clarity. She knew of only one way a prisoner could get out that fast.

Kane watched the color drain from her face. He had expected her to be surprised, but she looked as if she'd just received the scare of her life. "Are you okay?" he asked.

She knew she ought to do something, but what? Dial 911? Race outside and flag down the first motorist who came along? She tried to move, but her feet felt as though they'd been set in cement.

An escaped convict in Hardeeville? Was it possible?

Kane watched, transfixed, as Melanie

Abercrombie's eyes glazed over, and then rolled back in her head like dice in a card game. She swayed, and he reached for her. He wasn't fast enough. She collapsed and fell against a box of drain cleaner with the grace and finesse of a hundred-pound gunny sack of Vidalia onions.

To get free excerpts and news about Charlotte and her newest projects, become a charter member of her readers club at https://authorfriendly.leadpages.net/listexcerpt/